PIXELS AND POLTERGEISTS

PIXELS AND POLTERGEISTS

PENNY AND BOOTS™ BOOK THREE

AMY HOPKINS

MICHAEL ANDERLE

LMBPN Publishing
PMB 196, 2540 South Maryland Pkwy
Las Vegas, NV 89109

First US edition, December 2019
eBook ISBN: 978-1-64202-628-3
Print ISBN: 978-1-64202-629-0

THE PIXELS AND POLTERGEISTS TEAM

Thanks to the JIT Readers

Rachel Beckford
Jackey Hankard-Brodie
Diane L. Smith
Jeff Eaton
Deb Mader
Misty Roa
Paul Westman
Angel LaVey
Kelly O'Donnell
Debi Sateren
Dave Hicks
Larry Omans

If I've missed anyone, please let me know!

Editor
SkyHunter Editing Team

To Peanut Butter. Thank you for being the cutest fluff I've ever seen. For the last eight months you've been a companion, support pupper, hole-digging-helper and inefficient babysitter. I love you, boy. Sorry for getting your balls cut off.

— Amy

*To Family, Friends and
Those Who Love
to Read.
May We All Enjoy Grace
to Live the Life We Are
Called.*

— Michael

Penny lifted the scarf around her neck so that it covered her nose. It didn't work. The cloying aroma of cinnamon drowned her senses.

She glanced to one side, where Amelia clutched a handkerchief to her face, her eyes red and watering.

Penny shook her head. Amelia jerked her shoulders in a desperate shrug. Penny waved her hands and mouthed, "*No!*"

Tears streamed from Amelia's eyes. A frantic look was growing on the girl's face.

Seeing what was to come, Penny cowered.

Amelia sneezed, and a screech filled the air as the ragged bird at the top of the mountain of twigs, sticks, incense, and various spices raised its angry head. Black, beady eyes stared at the cluster of bushes that hid Penny and Amelia.

"Now you've gone and done it." Cisco's voice was hushed, but clearly audible through the tiny earbud Penny wore.

"I couldn't help it," Amelia hissed. It was a mistake. The quick intake of breath that fed her words set off a loud coughing spasm. "Oh, no."

"Duck!" Before the word was out of Penny's mouth, she rolled to one side. A wisp of hair tickled her face as the angry bird dove between them.

It squawked again, then hacked a limp cough of its own. The bird spat and shook its wings, dislodging a few worn feathers. Not many remained—the bird looked scrawny and decrepit. With a haughty glare, it waddled back to its funeral pyre.

"Have you untangled that net yet?" Penny grumbled into her microphone. "If we don't catch that damned phoenix before it ignites, this whole forest is going to go up in flames."

"I'm trying, I'm trying." The urgency in Cisco's voice rang true. "The bird really made a mess of it, though."

"I told you, you were holding it wrong," Red chimed in. "You need to hold your hand the other way around."

"Yeah?" Cisco sounded heated now. "I didn't see your hairy ass running to help me when the claws of doom were trying to gouge out my eyeballs."

Penny groaned. "It's a geriatric featherball, Cisco. Can you just catch it already? I've got dirt in my eyes, incense up my nose, and leaves in my crack. This was supposed to be an easy assignment, not a trip to Hell and back."

"I thought you were on my side!" In his frustration, Cisco forgot he was supposed to be staying quiet. Penny could hear the echo of his voice from the other side of the pile of debris.

The phoenix perked its head up from the cluster of

twigs it was rearranging at the top of the bird-made mountain. It spread its wings and a few more feathers were plucked out by the errant breeze, leaving ominous gaps in the once strong wings. The bird took a step, then another. It gave a tiny hop, probably intending to launch itself into the air.

Instead, it tripped.

With a rustling landslide of nesting material, the phoenix rolled to the bottom of the pile. It lifted a dazed head, hiccupped, and burst into flames.

"Shit." Penny scrambled backward as a rush of heat fanned her face. She took a deep breath, trying not to choke on the fine clouds of scented ash as she yelled for backup. "*Boots*! You're up! Code—uh—Twelve? Seventeen?"

"Fuck the code, just bring the rain, Princess." Amelia turned a frantic grin Penny's way. She lifted both hands in a "what are you gonna do" gesture.

"What she said." Penny edged back from the roaring fire as dry leaves began to ignite around them, floating into the air and drifting into the surrounding forest. "Come on, Boots. We don't have all day!"

Her plea was answered with a deep gurgling sound. She glanced over her shoulder and bit down on an instinctive urge to scream.

The fat snake that meandered toward them looked nothing like her longtime friend. Far from the slender, rainbow rope who spent most of her time lazily coiled in one of Penny's knapsacks, this monstrosity dragged itself between the trees like a legless buffalo.

"Better get out of the way, Penny!" Amelia grabbed Penny's arm and guided her away from the pudgy, dazed serpent. "You haven't seen what happens when she opens her mouth. I have!"

Penny couldn't resist watching over her shoulder as she let Amelia drag her back. The snake's fat body had swollen enough that Penny almost couldn't see over her back. Despite Boots' monstrous size, it wasn't until she let the water out that Penny realized just how much she had ingested.

To say that the water rushed from the serpent's mouth would be an understatement. Exploded, flooded, pummeled, perhaps. Boots did her best to direct the spray at the flaming funeral pyre of the phoenix. Somehow, Penny still got drenched. Clouds of steam plumed into the air, then coalesced into scalding raindrops that fell from the sky.

It took several minutes for the air to clear. Finally, Penny pulled free of Amelia's grasp.

"Spot fire!" Red called. His warning was followed by the hiss of the fire extinguisher.

Penny thought she spotted movement in the muddy ash and sludge ahead. "Cisco, do you still have the net?"—

She picked her way through carefully. Had it been her imagination? *No—there!* Penny pounced, trusting her instincts. She landed belly first in the sludge, but her groping hands quickly found what they were looking for. When she stood again, covered in a thick coating of wet ash, she held a tiny mass of wriggling, naked flesh in her hands. "Gotcha!"

She looked up at the sound of squelching footsteps to see Cisco and Red approaching.

"Aw, look at the wee beastie," Red cooed. He held out a

foil blanket. "Here you go. Wrap him up before he gets cold. Or sets something else on fire."

"I don't think he can, can he?" Amelia joined them, a large gilded cage in her arms. She set it down and unlatched the door. "I'm pretty sure he can only ignite when he's almost dead."

"*Almost* dead?" Cisco argued. "That bird looked like it had passed on in a retirement village, then stuck around as a moldering taxidermy project for another decade after." He helped Penny settle the bird in the cage, then locked it and eyed Penny. "When Red said he'd planned a dirty weekend, I assumed he was talking about Amelia."

Cisco yelped as the two women punched him, but managed a limp high five with Red afterward.

"I do need a shower," Penny admitted. She glared at the bird. "You know, this all could have gone down a lot easier if you had just cooperated."

Chirp.

"Where did Boots go?" Cisco looked around, a hint of worry lacing his voice.

"She's probably sleeping it off," Penny said.

She had thoroughly researched Boots' water abilities before the mission, helped by the information her friends had gleaned from the serpent's appearance when Penny had fought the Kraken. Her task was made even easier by several new reports of Rainbow Serpent sightings back in Australia. In fact, one had taken up a mascot position at a local fire station.

The serpent—named Monty by the local brigade—had helped put out a couple of bush fires and even saved a young child from a burning house. The reports lodged by the regional investigators had all confirmed that after a "major water event," the serpent in question would disappear for a day or two, returning no worse for wear to resume its duties as a volunteer fire-fighter.

Seeing Penny's confidence brought a grin to Cisco's face. "I guess we're done, then. We'll drop off this little squawker and then head to Paddy's?"

"Not until I've cleaned up," Penny remarked dryly. "Unless you want me to dump a bucket of slurry in *your* pants so you can see how it feels?"

"You can get in my pants any—" Cisco's quip was cut short by a sharp slap on the back of his head.

"Don't get too far ahead of yourself," Penny warned him. "We had *one* date. Well, three-quarters of a date. And even if it wasn't interrupted by a crazy emergency, doesn't mean anything was going to happen after."

"You didn't tell me anything about that," Amelia broke in. "When you got in so late last night, I just assumed you and Cisco had been getting frisky in his room."

"If that was the case, love, I'd have come to visit you." Red leaned past Penny's scarlet face and winked at his girlfriend.

Cisco shuddered. "It was awful. Not the date!" he explained hastily. "The Myther."

Amelia spread her hands, waiting expectantly.

Penny sighed. "Remember that old urban legend about a woman who had hippy dreadlocks for so long, a spider laid eggs in it?"

"Yeah, sure," Amelia replied. Then, her eyes grew large. "Nooo."

"Yup." Penny's stomach roiled just thinking about it.

"They were climbing down her face, and chunks of hair and scalp were falling away."

"No way!" Amelia squealed, waving away any attempt Penny might make to continue. "Don't tell me anymore. That poor woman!"

"Not a woman," Cisco corrected. "One of the agents stationed at the hospital sent me a text this morning. They tested the body, she had no DNA."

"She DIED?" Amelia gasped. "I don't care if she was real-real or a construct, that's awful!"

Penny nodded. Though the concept of Mythers and the study they did made them seem like ephemeral beings, her relationship with many of them—Boots, Paddy, Bacchus—had her questioning that. Paddy could feel pain, so could Boots. That woman, 'real' or not, had suffered.

Penny shook off her melancholy. Right now, they had a job to do. "Come on. Let's get this little firebug out of here." She grabbed the cage and headed back for the van, dragging it awkwardly beside her.

A moment later, the other side of the cage lifted. Cisco smiled at Penny. "Need a lift?"

"Thanks." Penny gave him a warm grin. "You know, dinner was really nice. We should do it again."

Cisco glanced away but couldn't hide his widening grin. "Really?"

"Really."

CHAPTER TWO

"It's quiet in here tonight," Cisco commented as they walked through the door of Paddy's Irish Bar.

Penny nodded. She'd picked up a few extra shifts over the break between semesters and had gotten used to the ebb and flow of customers throughout the week. "Tuesdays are the easy nights. The Mythers like to catch up on Mondays, the Protectorate—that's the angel and godmother alliance I was telling you about—hold meetings here on Wednesdays, and the regular crowd comes in from Thursday to Sunday. Tuesday is the only night I don't have to break up some kind of barney." She paused, remembering one evening a few weeks ago when two humans had started a fight over a girl. "Well, most Tuesdays."

Amelia cocked an eyebrow. "Barney?"

"It's a fight, love." Red winked at Penny. "I really do need to teach you proper English."

"Hey, Paddy!" Penny raised a hand to wave at the leprechaun, who hurried over.

"Penny! Did ye get your schedule yet?" He thrust a half-empty drink in her hand. "Here's a whiskey. Quick, down the hatch. Ye really need to go get that schedule for me, Paddy is on me arse about it." He waggled his hands, shooing her away. "Go on, off with ye. I don't want ta see ye back until ye have it."

Frowning, Penny dug around in her purse. "I've got a copy right here." She held out a slip of paper. "I emailed it to Josh yesterday. Didn't he get it?"

"Oh. Uh…" Paddy glanced around frantically. "He must have forgotten to tell me. But really, all of ye should be goin' just the same."

"Why?" Penny set the glass on a nearby table and folded her arms. "Paddy, what's going on?"

"Can't a leprechaun have a drink in peace?" Paddy folded his arms defiantly. "One night of quiet, that's all I be wantin'."

Red laid his accent on thick, his face the very picture of disapproval. "Now, Paddy, I can't believe ye'd kick out a fellow countryman."

Paddy looked over his shoulder, then back at Penny. "It's…um, school. That's it. Yer in school, all of ye, and it's yer first week back and—"

"PADDYYYYYY!" The howl was muffled but still held a painful note that set Penny's teeth on edge.

Red clutched his ears. "What in the hells?"

"Paddy! You can't run from me!" A small, elderly woman hobbled out of the back room and glowered at the leprechaun. "How *could* you? I *trusted* you!" She threw a tiny object at the subject of her ire. It bounced off his hat and pinged on the floor.

Penny stooped down carefully to pick it up, unwilling to take her eyes off the woman. "It's a ring." She held it up to the light. "It's…plastic? Costume jewelry."

At that, the woman burst into mournful tears, her pitch rising as she began to keen.

"Paddy?" Cisco cleared his throat and spoke louder to be heard over the ruckus. "Paddy, what did you do?"

Paddy stared at the floor glumly, hands behind his back. He mumbled something inaudible.

"Excuse me, miss?" Red approached the tiny, howling woman. She stopped mid-cry and glared up at him with wet eyes. "Do you need some help?"

"Help? Yes." Her lips curled back in an ugly grimace, but she lowered her voice to an angry hiss. "You can bring your fur and teeth out to disembowel this trickster beast, savage his throat, then bury what's left of him twenty feet under the soil."

"Uh… Anything else?" Red stepped back, unnerved.

The woman straightened. "I'll pay you well. Really, name your price." She reached up to pat her grey hair back into place, then tugged the front of her dress to smooth it.

Red coughed, turning to mouth at Penny with pleading eyes. "*Help.*"

Penny sighed. "Listen, lady, we're not going to hurt Paddy. Well, not *that* badly, anyway." She shot the leprechaun in question a warning glance, willing him to keep his mouth shut. "How about you tell us what's wrong, and we'll see if we can't make it better without killing anyone."

"What's wrong?" The woman spat on the floor, and Penny made a mental note have the bar staff clean it up before someone slipped—or in case it was poisonous. "He's a lying, scheming little gombeen, that's what's wrong."

"What's a gombeen?" Amelia whispered.

"*He's* a gombeen!" The woman stepped forward and thrust a finger toward Paddy. This close, her resolve shattered and tears welled again. "He promised me he'd treat me well. That he wouldn't abandon me like the others did. He said he'd shower me with gifts and buy me a wee cottage to live in, far away from all the hateful humans who curse me and call me horrible things."

Understanding dawned and Penny rounded on Paddy, who had started to inch toward the door. "Oh, no, you don't, you little shit. Explain. *Now!*"

Paddy gave a deep sigh. "Aye, I did ye wrong, Orlagh. I did *mean* to keep me promises, but me gold… Well, I can't just be *givin'* it away."

Penny stared at him. "You cheap, weaselly little—"

Paddy raised his hands defensively. "I can't be helpin' it! I'm a leprechaun. I can't stop bein' greedy any more than Red can stop sproutin' fur on a full moon."

"And what are you?" Penny asked the tiny old woman. Orlagh was too short to be a regular human.

Orlagh lifted her chin, then raised a hand to pull a fine cloth veil over her face. She didn't speak until it was secure, and even then, she kept her voice low as if she were afraid of being overheard. "Your people know me as Banshee. Though they call me much worse."

Even with her face hidden, Orlagh's pain shone through in her words.

Penny walked over to kneel before her. "Orlagh, you seem like a lovely person. I'm sorry Paddy took advantage of you. If it helps, I think he's telling the truth when he says he can't help it." She waited, breath held.

Orlagh gave a slow nod. "It is his nature. I should have known better."

"To make it right, Paddy will buy you that cottage." Penny ignored the outraged screech from behind. "Somewhere nice and secluded, and far from anyone that would hurt you. There are reserves being set up to protect your people—perhaps we can find a place for you in one of them. I'll make sure you're safe."

Orlagh dipped her head, and when she raised it again, the veil had fallen. Her face glowed with youthful beauty and her eyes glittered over a small smile. It was suddenly clear how Paddy had fallen in love with her. "Thank you. Your honor shall be spoken among the dead for eternity."

"Oh. That's, um, nice." Penny glanced back at Paddy, jabbing a finger in his direction. "And *you* are never going to make false promises again."

Paddy grumbled, snorted, and eventually nodded. "Fine." He toed the floor for a moment before raising plaintive eyes. "But if you're stayin', can I have me whiskey back?"

* * *

Chastened by the harsh talking to, Paddy declined Penny's offer to join them for drinks. "I'll go give ye schedule to Paddy. Ye know, just in case that email didn't get through." He stalked off, throwing one last cautionary glance at the door Orlagh had given a mighty slam when she had left.

"Who would have thought Paddy would fall for a

banshee," Amelia mused. "Not that she wasn't beautiful. I just assumed he was so in love with himself he'd never notice another person."

"I guess even Paddy gets lonely sometimes," Red guessed. "But what a prick, promising the lass a house then giving her a plastic ring!"

Amelia gave him a pointed look. "Yeah, a total dick move. If you ever pull something like that, I'll—"

"Never!" Red leaned over to give her a wet kiss on the cheek. "I'd never treat my girl like that."

"Is that because you love her, or because you're suitably scared of her?" Cisco asked.

Red shrugged. "Can't it be both?" He dodged Amelia's swat.

Shaking his head at their antics, Cisco shifted in his seat to face Penny. "Are you going to Glass' class first thing tomorrow?"

The defense instructor, disgusted with the physical shortcomings of his students, had scheduled several extra classes during the week. The dean had refused to make them mandatory, much to his disappointment, but it seemed most of the students in Penny's class had taken up the offer.

She nodded. "We've got Cyber, then Greek *and* British mythology all stacked in a row. I'll need the workout to get me through it without going crazy."

Cisco groaned in agreement. "The schedule is full-on this semester."

"Aye, but at least the gang is back together!" Red grinned.

He, Amelia, Penny, and Cisco had all chosen the Greek and British history specializations. Penny had signed up for a third—the Australasian mythology branch. But she would be taking that class alone.

"Why did they make Cybermythology a mandatory subject, though?" Amelia happily accepted the plate of wings a waitress brought over. "Seems more like something Trevor would be into."

"They probably don't want to lose all the students to hoaxes personified," Cisco replied. "I still can't believe Penny turned down a prince."

"At least I know I have a backup if you ever turn me down." Penny tipped her head toward the door. "Or if you turn out to be an ass like Paddy."

Cisco snorted. "If you believe there's a chance of either, then you don't know me at all. Do you really think my mother would raise someone like that?"

Chuckling, Penny shook her head. "Good point. Maybe we could get her to teach Paddy some morals?"

"Paddy has morals!" The leprechaun in question emerged from the back room brandishing Penny's schedule, which was now stapled to a second sheet of paper. "Old Paddy is almost done, but he needs to see ye in the office."

Penny nodded and hurried over. She shoved through the swinging door and took a hard left to arrive in Joshua's office. "You needed to see me?" she asked.

"Yeah." Joshua's desk was cluttered with invoices and empty coffee mugs. "I know you said the Friday night class was optional, but I wanted to make sure you're really okay with missing it. I hate to ask, but that's our worst night on the floor and you're so damn good at what you do."

Penny grinned. "You're damn right, I am. And I know Friday sucks. That's why I circled it three times and noted that I could be flexible there. It's just basic fitness, entirely optional, and I can make the time up in the Academy gym during the week."

"Okay. If you're certain." Joshua passed Penny a neatly typed roster. "Thanks, Penny."

"Joshua?" Penny hesitated before leaving. "You've got access to all Paddy's financials, right?"

"Not all." Joshua leaned back in his chair and rubbed his face. It was almost as if he could sense the bad news coming. "Just his bank accounts. I'm sure he's got a stash of gold somewhere he hasn't told me about. Why?"

"I'm sure Paddy himself will fill you in," Penny told him. "But just in case, you'll need to organize a real estate purchase for him."

"What has he done this time?" Joshua asked the question with an air of well-worn patience.

Penny gave him the short version. "He wooed a banshee and made her a promise he knew he wasn't planning to keep."

"And now the little shit wants me to clean up his mess?" Joshua shook his head. "He knows he needs to keep his head down. This court case of his is gaining steam—and a lot of opposition. Does he really think something like this won't bring unwanted attention?"

"He's an idiot," Penny agreed. "But he's our friend. I don't want him to get eaten, or whatever it is a banshee does to her victims."

Joshua drummed his fingers on his desk. "More than anything, I don't want to mop up the remains. I'll get on it."

"Thanks, Josh." Penny sighed with relief. "I knew I could count on you."

CHAPTER THREE

Penny slid behind a desk next to Cisco, fanning her face. "Are my cheeks still flushed?" she asked.

Fitness class that morning had been brutal. Apparently, Glass was determined to make up for any loss of strength and stamina the students had suffered over the break between semesters.

"You look fine," Cisco assured her. "Better than Red, anyway."

"What?" Red snapped. "How was I supposed to know he'd have us doing PACER testing? I went for a bloody run before class, didn't I?"

His outburst was interrupted by the arrival of the Greek History professor. Penny watched as the teacher, a grey-haired man with a clean-shaven face and buttoned cardigan, carefully unpacked a stack of history texts onto his desk. As she watched him straighten his books, her brain gave a nudge. "Cisco, does he look familiar to you?"

"Nope. Not to me." Cisco leaned over to peer into Penny's bag. "Hey, you don't have a—"

He grinned when Penny whipped out a notebook for him and barked a laugh when he saw the cover. *"Power Rangers?"*

"You have no idea how hard that was to find." Penny dug a pen out for him. "The pink ranger was sold out everywhere!"

"I love you, Penny!" Cisco beamed up at her, a flush creeping onto his face as he realized what he'd said. "I mean… I didn't mean…"

"It's okay," Penny assured him. "I know I'll always take second place to the first love of your life." She flicked a finger toward the cartoon ranger.

"Uh-huh." Cisco buried himself in the notebook, writing out the lesson name in cramped handwriting. *Greek History and Mythology.*

"This class is packed," Penny commented as the students filed in. It was the first time she had seen a room filled at the Academy. "I wonder how much of that has to do with Bacchus?"

"All of it," Cisco admitted. "Mom said they almost had to split the class into two sessions."

Penny opened her mouth to respond but stopped, grinning as Amelia stepped into the room.

"Hey, Mr. Hardwick!" Amelia gave the professor a brief hug. "Gerry didn't tell me you took the teaching job."

A flash of understanding hit Penny as she realized why the professor looked so familiar. He bore a strong resemblance to his son, Gerry.

"It was a last-minute decision." Prof Hardwick patted Amelia on the shoulder and gestured to a nearby desk. "I'm glad to see your punctuality has improved over the years, if only by a little."

Amelia didn't take offense at the jibe, hurrying toward the seat the professor had pointed to. Penny realized it was the only free desk in the room.

Red caught Penny's glance and shrugged. "I told her I wouldn't save her a spot if she was late," he explained.

"Is that really Gerry's dad?" Cisco asked. "Gerry from the party?"

"What party?" Red gave him a quizzical glance. "Who's Gerry?"

"You don't remember?" Cisco shook his head, bemused. "I know Bacchus did a number on your memory that night, but I didn't realize you'd forgotten it completely."

Red's confused shrug gave Penny a jolt of surprise. "Can you not remember anything about the party? We went to Gerry's and Bacchus appeared. That was the first time we met him."

Red shrugged again. "I remember Amelia telling me about it. That's about it." He waved away Penny's concerns. "Don't worry, I already spoke to old party pants about it. He thinks the magic amnesia spell left a residue and it conflicted with my wolf magic. Amelia said she only noticed the gap in my memory after I got turned. He offered to fix it, but I didn't really want him digging around in my head again."

Penny sighed with frustration. "Sure, it's only your brain. It's not like anything can go wrong."

Red laughed. "It's just a bit of memory loss. Don't worry yourself about it."

If she had to be honest, she *wasn't* worried, not if

Bacchus had already assured Red he was fine. Though Penny had been dubious of Bacchus's motives at first, she had come to trust the ancient philosopher.

Their conversation was halted by the beginning of class. Professor Hardwick did indeed introduce himself as Gerry's dad. Apparently, Amelia and her friends weren't the only ones who had attended one of the god-fueled parties. Hardwick explained that he had always been a Greek history professor. With the tearing of the Veil, all his impossible dreams of meeting the ancient Greek deities had been realized.

"I bet that's who your mum was talking about when we covered veil acceptance back in our first semester," Penny murmured to Cisco.

Madera had spent an entire class on the vagaries of who could see Mythers, who could learn to see them, and why it seemed some people would spend the rest of their lives insisting the tearing of the veil was one giant hoax despite the swathes of evidence staring them in the face.

During her explanation, she had referenced a colleague who, though well past middle age, had been able to see the Mythers from his very first encounter. She had used this friend as an example of how, although most adults needed several exposures to Mythers in life-threatening circumstances in order to see them consistently, some adults were a bit, well, special.

Although Madera hadn't come out and said it, Penny had gained the impression that she had used the word "special" in place of "gullible."

"What? I thought she was talking about Agent Crenel."

Cisco's pen continued to scratch in his notebook as he spoke.

Penny snorted. "No, he had to learn the hard way. He didn't tell you about the incident with the harpy?"

Red put a finger to his lips. "Shh, he's about to get to the bit where Cronos eats all his babies."

"Gross." Penny jotted down the information anyway. "Why would he want to meet someone like *that*?"

"One of the babies was Zeus." Cisco shrugged. "He seemed pretty cool."

"Zeus is a dirty old man. He even tried to hit on Vila the other day." Penny paused. "Wait a minute, if Cronos ate Zeus, then how did Zeus become the top god?"

Cisco rolled his eyes and gestured to the front of the class, where Professor Hardwick was, indeed, explaining how Zeus became *Zeus*. By the end of the lesson, Penny realized her knowledge of the Greek gods was more than lacking. Not only that, but this particular branch of mythology wasn't just made up of easy-going party gods and horny old men. She shuddered to think what would happen if some of the less friendly Titans were to appear in the world.

Hardwick had wrapped up the class by jotting the names of the legendary Greeks who were confirmed to have crossed through the veil. After that, his excitement had faltered. "There are claims, my dear children, that the veil was not just torn once. It is continuing to tear. As the rift widens, so does the mythological populace that exists in our world. As wonderful as it is to converse with ancient philosophers and play with forgotten magicks, we must always bear in mind the threat that this poses."

He dismissed the class, turning his back on the evacuating students to clean the whiteboard.

Penny shared a worried glance with Cisco. "Wow. That ended on a downer."

Unperturbed, Red quickly stacked his books, put away his pens, and hurried over to Amelia. She slapped his chest, and he grimaced.

"You were supposed to save me a seat!" She made a slight gesture with her hand when he tried to speak. "Don't even pretend I was late. I got here a whole minute before class started!"

Chagrined, Red hung his head in shame. "Sorry love. Won't happen again."

Amelia grinned. "At the very least, you owe me a drink. I'm going to need it once today is over!"

Penny inhaled deeply, savoring the aroma of freshly ground coffee. It was Wednesday, and she had grabbed Cisco and headed straight to Tony's cafe after their morning class for a desperately needed hit of caffeine.

Her brain still hurt from the previous day's lessons. They had covered Greek, British, and Cyber myths, the classes running until seven the previous evening. Heading out to Paddy's to wind down after the long day had been a mistake, she decided.

Waking up to a legal class had been the last straw. A steamer hissed and Penny winced, head pounding. "You know what? Just give me the biggest coffee you've got. With lots of sugar."

Hssss. Penny's backpack wriggled.

"Sorry. And a bowl of milk for Boots." Penny massaged a temple as she handed over her credit card to Violet, the barista.

"I thought *last* semester was tough," Cisco groaned. He held two fingers up, signaling to Violet that he would have whatever caffeine-laden monstrosity she was making for Penny. "This week has been hell, and it's not even over. We still have one more class tomorrow. I've never been so glad for an afternoon off!"

"Speak for yourself." Penny moved away from the counter to find them a table in the quiet café. "I have Australasian Myth and Legend tonight. For some reason, I thought taking an extra class would be a great idea."

"You're a sucker for punishment. I bet it won't be as bad as the Great Britain Mythology class, though. Robbins has the personality of a wet sock." Cisco let Penny wave him away from the pastry cabinet.

"Pick a table," she demanded. "My legs still feel like they're going to give out after Glass' thrashing yesterday."

Cisco obliged, moving toward a booth. "Hey, what's that in the corner?" He pointed toward an arcade machine tucked in the corner of the coffee shop. "You want to check it out?"

Penny rolled her eyes but followed him over to the machine. The screen glowed as pixelated explosions erupted from one of the triangular ships darting to and fro across the screen. Below, a green ship flashed as a yellow blip hit it. A slow ding-dong played, and **Game Over** rolled over the screen before the demonstration began again.

Cisco dug in his pocket but pulled out an empty hand with a crestfallen expression. "Got any quarters?"

"Nope." Penny didn't even have to look. She had lost every cent in her purse trying to outsmart Paddy in a game of poker the night before. Between the nineteen dollars and twenty-five cents lost to the cheating leprechaun, and the mild hangover she had woken up to in the morning, her visit to the bar had been one she would rather forget. "And despite always threatening to turn Boots into a purse, I don't think she carries money."

Teeth grazed Penny's earlobe as the offended snake let her know what she thought about Penny's purse idea.

Cisco tapped the plastic buttons absentmindedly. He snatched his hand back when Boots darted forward with an angry hiss. Her face struck his wrist, knocking it away from the machine.

"Boots!" Penny grabbed Boots and tried to shove the writhing snake back into her bag. "What the hell has gotten into you? Sorry, Cisco."

"It's fine." Cisco rubbed his arm. "She didn't bite me. She probably just knows how bad I suck at Space Invaders."

When they were settled at a table, Penny let Boots emerge from her backpack. The serpent slowly crept out toward Cisco and nuzzled his arm apologetically.

"What was that all about?" Penny asked gently. She had never known Boots to strike out like that.

Boots responded by rising up and baring her fangs at the arcade machine.

"It's a game," Penny told her firmly. "There aren't *actually* aliens in the box, dumbo."

Boots flopped onto the table, turning away from Penny in a huff.

When Tony himself delivered the coffees to their table, Penny asked him about the arcade game.

"It was a deal I couldn't refuse." He shrugged. "A guy in a suit came in, paid me $1500 to let him install it, and said I can keep all the profits." He spread his hands at Penny's frown. "I know, I know. It's too good to be true, and it'll probably come back to bite me in the ass later. I needed the money, though. It's been quiet around here lately."

Penny resolved to ask Bacchus to make a casual appearance at the small café. The god owed her a favor for tipping him off about some trouble that was brewing in the courts regarding food licenses for magically conjured beverages, and simply showing his face at a venue would have customers frequenting the shop for weeks to come. From there, Tony's friendly staff and awesome coffee would be enough to sustain things.

The door chime jingled as a group of customers wandered in, and Tony hurried back to the coffee machine.

"It's gotta be a scam," Penny murmured to Cisco. "Doesn't it?"

Cisco shrugged. "Sure, but I don't see what they're after. The machines don't take credit cards, so there are no skimmers installed. And it's old, like, Eighties old."

"Oh, you know that because you were around back then?" Penny teased.

"The Eighties are cool again. I'm cool. Therefore, I know all about the Eighties." Cisco frowned. "Though I haven't come across that particular game before. What is it called again? *Polybius?*"

CHAPTER FOUR

When Penny arrived at her Australasian mythology class that evening, it was empty. She quickly pulled out her phone and brought up the email the Academy had sent with her schedule.

"Classroom four, six PM, Thursdays with Professor Steele." Penny glanced at the room number and her watch to confirm the details as she read them out. "I'm in the right place. Why isn't anyone else here?"

"Because you're the only student enrolled."

Penny spun toward the voice, an overwhelming rush of comfort enveloping her at the sound of a familiar accent. *Not quite Aussie, but Kiwis are practically family.*

The professor for Australian Mythological Studies reminded Penny of her English teacher in high school. Grey hair pulled back in a tight bun, fine lines at the corners of her mouth, and a 'don't fuck with me' glint to her eye.

Despite that, Steele smiled. "I know. I don't look like

much. Still, would have been nice to have more than one student enrolled in the class."

"I don't think it's personal," Penny quickly assured her. "There was a lot to choose from."

"Oh, don't worry about it." Steele unlocked the classroom and pushed open the door. "Seeing as it's just us, where do you want to begin?"

"Well, how about here?" Penny loosened the top of her backpack.

Boots emerged, sleepy-eyed from her afternoon nap. She tested the air with her tongue and perked up at seeing the professor.

"Oh! I'd heard rumors about your little friend. She's a rainbow?" Steele leaned down to scratch Boots between the eyes, and the snake gave a smooth purr. "Wow, a real live Dreamtime legend. She sounds like a cat!"

"Sounds like a cat, ego like a cat..." Penny ignored Boots' offended cough. "I've read everything I can on the Serpent and on the Dreamtime. I took this class, hoping you'd know more than the books."

Steele gave a small smile. "Dear, I spent six years in your country. For most of that, I was living out bush with the caretakers of the land. I learned things you won't find in *any* book, so I daresay I can help. But let's start by seeing what you already know, hey?"

Despite Steele's gentle manner, she grilled Penny relentlessly, asking her questions about the stories and legends she'd researched, the symbolism she'd investigated, and more than anything else, about how it all linked back to Boots.

She asked about Boots' behavior, her diet, her sleeping habits. She even examined Boots, asking her to perform tasks like stretch out into a line or find the pink ball in a box of multicolored ping pongs. Boots completed each task with enthusiasm.

"Incredible," Steele breathed. "What about water? Healing? What magic have you seen her do?"

"She can suck up loads of water and expel it," Penny told her. "That's about it, I think?" Boots gave her tail a haughty twitch. "Not that a rainbow firehose isn't spectacular in its own right," Penny teased.

In response, Boots turned her head away from Penny and slithered over to Professor Steel, who sat cross-legged on the floor, surrounded by ping pong balls. The snake flopped into her lap with an offended snort.

"She understands you so well." Steele jotted another note down as the snake wrapped herself into a tight coil. "And she exhibits almost human emotion."

"*Almost* human?" Penny cocked an eyebrow. "You haven't seen her response when I tell her to get her own bowl of milk. It's like I've insulted her newborn child!"

Steele added another note with a flourish. "Has she bred?"

Penny blinked. "No. Can she?"

"There's no reason she couldn't." Steele leaned back in her chair, fingers steepled beneath her chin. "Has she ever been given the opportunity?"

Penny looked at the serpent, who lifted her head and cocked it to one side. *Like a puppy*, Penny thought. *Or a curious child.*

"I don't even know how old she is," Penny admitted. "Most snakes take a while to mature enough for that, don't they?"

"She wasn't born the day you found her, Penny," Steele corrected gently. "She's an ancient being, from a land that not only accepts her but one she was literally made for. Over here? She's away from her own kind and from the legends that created her."

"She's got me." Penny bit her lip and tried to sound less defensive. "I didn't mean to bring Boots here. She snuck into my luggage. I'm not even sure how she made it past customs without anyone noticing her."

"Ah."

Though the professor made a show of dropping the subject, Penny was left feeling discomfited by the exchange even as the topic of conversation moved onto more mundane things, like drop bears, bunyips, and Maori gods.

When the lesson was over, Penny headed back to their room despite her growling stomach.

She gently placed Boots on her bed. "Can we talk, Boots?"

Boots stretched lazily, then rose up to flick a tongue on Penny's cheek.

"Are you happy here?" Penny asked.

Boots nodded eagerly.

Penny couldn't resist reaching out a hand for Boots to nuzzle. "Are you lonely?"

Boots snorted, a sound she had perfected over the previous months despite Penny's conviction that, according to serpentine anatomy, shouldn't be possible.

Boots twisted away, leaning over to Penny's bedside table. With gentle teeth, the snake picked up a photograph propped against a ballerina ornament. She dropped it in Penny's lap.

A soft smile touched Penny's lips as she looked at the image. "I know we have some amazing friends here."

It was a polaroid, taken at Paddy's. She, Cisco, Amelia, and Red had all posed with whiskey shots on Saint Patrick's day. Boots had draped herself over Penny's shoulders for the photo, and Paddy had somehow, despite being on the other side of the room moments before, photobombed the shot, his green hat and an empty glass taking up one corner of the frame.

Penny set the photo on the bed and gently pulled Boots' face to look at her. "They're not serpents, though. Don't you miss your own kind?"

Boots shook her head. Then, she bumped her head on Penny's chin before lowering herself to the ground.

As Penny trailed Boots down to the dining hall, she tried to reassure herself that Boots wouldn't lie to her. Still, a germ of unease had settled in her gut, and Penny knew it wouldn't be banished easily.

Four days later and Penny was still stuck on Professor Steele's words. Glass noticed her mood during the fitness class Monday evening, calling her out after she landed a frustrated right hook on Jason's jaw during a sparring session.

"Jason, go to the first aid room. Penny, you're out for the night." Waving away her stricken apology for hurting a fellow student, Glass added, "Six AM tomorrow, here, for a catch-up lesson. You can get out whatever is bothering you against someone who doesn't block hits like a drunken four-year-old."

"Hey!" Jason turned as he reached the doorway. "I'm still here, you know."

"No point being offended at the honest truth." Glass waved him away, then eyeballed Penny. "Go on, take the evening off and come back tomorrow. Don't be late."

Some of Penny's frustration had worn off after that class, and when Penny arrived in Glass's training room the next morning, she walked in with another apology on her lips.

"Don't say it," Glass warned her. "He deserved it. You were itching for a fight last night, but his head was in the damn clouds. Distracted by some girl, probably. We're not here to give each other manicures. He deserved what he got."

"Oh." She'd been too wrapped up in her own angst to notice at the time, but now Glass had pointed it out, Penny realized Jason had been more distracted than usual.

"How do you want to do this?" Glass tipped his head toward the wall of weapons.

Penny ran her eyes over the selection. "I haven't had a good sword fight in a while." The practice would do her good, and the added weight of chainmail armor—a prerequisite for fighting with the medieval weapons—might help her wear out the last of her jitters.

Glass nodded his acceptance. He walked to the armory cupboard and dragged out a suit for Penny. As she dressed, he donned his own equipment.

"What's got you so riled up?" he asked. "Wait, scratch that. If it's boy trouble, or hell, if it's girl trouble? I don't wanna know."

"It's snake trouble," Penny admitted. She stopped talking to pull a coif over her head. "Professor Steele kind of insinuated that Boots shouldn't be here, that she's better off with her own kind. Not that I had a choice in the matter—she came of her own accord."

But did she do that because she really wanted to, or just to make me happy?

"And what did Boots have to say about that?" Glass asked. He stood, rolling his shoulders to adjust to the weight of the armor.

Penny mimicked his actions, feeling comforted by the heavy mail draped over her torso and head. "She said she's happy here." Boots had made a big show of snuggling up to Amelia at dinner and even gave Cook a kiss on the cheek before they left the dining hall. "She says she's not lonely."

"Then why do you care?" Glass plucked a short sword from the stand and tossed it to Penny. "Do you think Steele is a threat?"

Penny caught the sword easily and twirled it in a circle. "A threat? Come on, Glass. It's not like she's going to steal a mythological creature and try to smuggle her home."

Glass pulled a second sword free, hefting it in his hand to test the weight. "Then my question stands. Why do you care?"

"She said Boots should breed!" Penny backed into the middle of the room, knowing that if she turned her back on Glass, he would take advantage of it even before their sparring officially began.

Glass laughed. "Jesus, Penny, you sound like an overprotective mother who doesn't want her kid to buy a motorbike."

"I do not." Penny knew she was beginning to sound petulant. She gripped her sword tighter and prepared to unleash her growing irritation on Glass.

"Saying she's mature isn't exactly an insult," Glass continued. "There are people on the streets calling Mythers the spawn of the devil. I don't see you getting all riled up about *them*." Glass moved into position.

Penny sank back into a defensive stance, holding her sword at the ready. "I don't have to sit through classes with *those* losers."

"You're deliberately missing my point." Glass struck without warning, the metallic clang of sword against sword echoing around the chamber. "Why. Do. You. Care?"

Penny grunted, parrying another strike. He had her on the back foot. She defended herself three more times before she found an opening. Penny thrust with her sword and Glass knocked it away easily. "Because I liked her. For about fifteen minutes, anyway."

"Why?" Glass followed his question with a flurry of sweeps and jabs.

Penny stumbled backward, already breathing hard. "She's from New Zealand. That's practically home. And she is a specialist in the mythological branch that created Boots. I thought Steele could tell me more about her, help me understand her. She wasn't supposed to suggest that I send Boots away."

"When did she say that?" Glass allowed her to regain her balance before striking again.

Penny grunted as she blocked a blow aimed at her knees. "She didn't."

"So you're mad because… Ah Hell, I don't even know what your problem is. You're putting words in her mouth and making assumptions based on your own misplaced guilt." Glass stepped back, allowing Penny to catch her breath. "You should be pissed, but not at her."

Penny huffed a quick breath. "When you put it like that, I feel like an idiot."

Glass lifted a shoulder. "You're not an idiot, but if you keep letting emotion fuck with your judgment, you'll pay the price eventually."

Penny raised an arm to wipe the sweat out of her eyes. *Thwack.* The flat of Glass's blade slapped against Penny's ribs, bruising them through the heavy mail.

"Ow! You bastard!" Penny stepped back, dropped her sword, and ripped the coif from her head, signaling the end of the match. "I learned my bloody lesson. Did you *have* to break a rib to drive it home?"

Glass smirked. "You didn't learn a damn thing. You're angry at *me* now, aren't you? You know better than to take your attention off an opponent, and you know better than to trust someone without a logical reason for doing so."

"Fuck you." Penny grinned to show the professor she held no hard feelings. "How about we try some hand to hand?"

"Giving up already?" Glass taunted. "I thought you needed the practice."

Penny groaned, knowing he was right. She took a deep breath. Her ribs complained, but not too badly. *They're not broken. No excuse.*

"Fine. Let's get it over with." She dropped the mail coif back on her head and picked the sword back up. "Bring it."

CHAPTER FIVE

"Do I want to see the other guy?" Cisco pushed open the coffee shop door for Penny, wincing at her black eye and the thin scratch on her cheek.

"Sadly, Professor Glass is fine." Penny grinned wryly. "The only damage I did to him was a busted knee. I made a real mess of it, too, bad enough that he sent me for the Asclepius staff."

"What, and he didn't let you use it?" Cisco let the door fall closed behind them. "What an asshole."

"He offered, I said no." Penny shrugged. "I only have a few bruises. It wouldn't be worth it."

Cisco frowned. "The staff is a bottomless pit of healing power. It's not like it runs out."

"It's not the only thing that's a bottomless pit right now." Penny pressed a hand to her stomach. "I skipped breakfast, then spent two hours working my ass off in the defense room. I could already eat a horse. The last thing I need is a magically-induced appetite boost."

"Oh. Then I guess we're ordering meals?" Cisco grinned and plucked a menu off a nearby table. "I was going to offer to pay, but I don't have enough for an actual horse."

Penny snorted. "I passed your mum on the way out. She was muttering something about 'young men begging for lunch money in their twenties.' I can pay my own way, thanks."

"That's a bit over-dramatic," Cisco replied. "All I asked is if she had a couple of quarters. I even gave her a dollar back. She made a profit!"

"Oh, for the game?" Penny glanced over at the arcade machine. Pixelated spaceships danced over the screen. "Can we eat first? I wasn't joking, I really am starving."

Cisco laughed. "Fine!" He dug his wallet out of a back pocket. "I meant it, by the way. Today's my shout… As long as you stick to burgers and coffee, not entire beasts of burden."

"A burger sounds perfect. Just get me the biggest one they've got, with a side of fries. And maybe a Coke?" Penny fished around for her own purse. "Here, let me give you some money. I was only teasing before. I don't actually want to send you broke."

Cisco put a hand up, refusing her offer. "Go find us a seat, I've got this."

Penny wandered over to the game and watched the scrolling screen. A triangular spaceship floated at the bottom, shooting beams of white at opposing ships and exploding them in a shower of red dots. The demo sequence ended, and a list of names scrolled up from the bottom.

1. Trevor White…… 52,559
2. Trevor White…… 47,331
3. Maximillian Bucks…… 30,000

The names continued down the list, all of them except the first three showing a score of five, ten, or twenty thousand.

"Hey, is that *Trevor* Trevor?" Cisco reached over Penny to point at the highest scorer. "His last name is White."

"Must be," Penny replied. "What about those other names? Joe King, Al E. Gator? They're too punny to be real." She ran her finger down the list.

Cisco laughed. "Nah, they're just placeholders. You can tell because the scores are all even multiples of a thousand."

"Ah." Interest already waning, Penny dropped her handbag on the table closest to the arcade machine. "You ordered?"

"Violet was out back. I'll do it now." He headed back for the register, where Violet had begun stacking paper coffee cups next to the espresso machine.

Penny sat just as the small bell over the coffee shop door jingled loudly and two heavyset men in crisp black suits barged in. Both had clean-shaven heads, dark sunglasses, and small black earbuds attached to cords leading inside their jackets. One pushed a dolly while the other ran his eyes over the cafe.

That doesn't seem normal. Although the men gave off an aura similar to agent Crenel and the rest of the CIA, something about these guys was a little off. Perhaps the way they moved in perfect unison, not speaking, not communicating, but somehow perfectly in sync. *Maybe they just look a little too much alike.* The men certainly looked similar enough to be brothers, and not just in their dress. Pale skin, ice-blue eyes, and perfectly straight noses gave them enough likeness that they could even be twins.

Her heart fluttered faster as the men approached her table. Behind them, Penny could see that Cisco had stopped mid-order, watching the men walking toward her.

Penny took a breath, preparing to give the men a friendly greeting. As she opened her mouth to speak, they brushed past her wordlessly. Without breaking stride, one of the men parked the dolly next to the arcade machine. The other smoothly knelt, inserted a key into the side, and dislodged a black box that jangled with quarters.

What the fuck? As strange as they looked for government employees, the idea of them working for a company selling old gaming machines would have made Penny laugh if she wasn't already so unsettled by their appearance.

The first man stooped over, withdrawing a small black box from one pocket. An attachment dangled from it that he plugged into the side of the arcade machine. Penny could see a small LED screen flare to life but couldn't make out what was on it. Before she could debate the safety of standing up to look, he unplugged it and shoved it back in his pocket. He grabbed the dolly, shoved it under the machine, and pushed it out of the shop.

The other man walked up to the counter and dropped the heavy box of coins on the counter. "You'll have a new machine first thing tomorrow." The man spoke in a clipped tone, his face expressionless as he turned away and walked out the door.

"Well, that was the weirdest thing I've ever seen," Cisco remarked when he joined Penny at her table. "Damn shame about the game, though. I was looking forward to having a go."

Penny twisted in her seat, trying to spot the duo out the window. She couldn't see them. "Really? Because that whole thing just made my skin crawl. Who were those guys?"

Cisco screwed up his face. "Guys like that are the reason conspiracy theories get started."

"That's the truth." When the bell jingled again, Penny's eyes shot to the door. "Oh, hey. Speak of the devil."

Trevor immediately went to the empty corner of the shop. "Damn."

"Nice to see you too, man," Cisco teased.

Trevor's head jerked up and he stammered an apology. "Sorry! I wasn't talking to you, I swear. I didn't even see you there."

"Sure, you didn't. I bet you—" Cisco yelped when Penny kicked him under the table.

"We know you didn't, Trevor." She kicked a seat out for him. "If you're looking for the arcade game, two goons just wheeled it away. They said something about a new one coming tomorrow."

Trevor let out a frustrated groan. "No! I thought they'd leave it here a bit longer, at least."

"We saw your high scores," Penny told him. "You really like space shooters, don't you?"

Trevor looked around the cafe, then ducked his head low. He cupped a hand over his mouth and whispered something too low for Penny to catch.

"What did you say?" She dropped her voice a little, but he hushed her anyway.

"Not so loud," he hissed. "I'm on an undercover operation." He darted another look around.

"You know," Cisco told him, his voice at a normal volume. "The worst way to avoid notice is looking like you're *trying* to avoid notice."

Trevor sat up and looked around again. With a chagrined expression, he settled back into his chair. "Oh."

"What are *you* doing on an op?" Penny asked. It was unusual to see anyone outside of the field agent track to be given a mission. Red and Amelia were only able to accompany Penny and Cisco out because of their track record with the Kraken from the first semester.

Grimacing, Trevor shook his head. "It's not official. Not yet, anyway. As soon as I've got enough evidence, though, I'm going straight to Agent Crenel. If I'm right, this will be huge!" His eyes grew big with excitement as he spoke.

"So… You're not gonna tell us what it is?" Cisco asked.

Trevor hesitated. Penny immediately began to reassure him that he didn't have to share, but he cut her off. "It's not that I don't trust you guys, really. I just don't want to put you in any danger."

Cisco smirked. "Well, Danger just happens to be my middle name."

"No, it's not." Penny snickered. "It's Bartholomew. Your mom told me that ages ago."

"My *other* middle name," Cisco said with a withering glare.

"Regardless," Penny continued patiently. "If Trevor doesn't want to tell us what he's working on, he doesn't have to. I'm sure he's got it under control." She shone a confident smile at Trevor, who blushed in return.

"Fine." Cisco twisted around to look over at Violet, who had two coffees and two burgers balanced on a tray. "Mmm, lunch is coming!"

Penny punctuated his statement with a loud stomach growl. The sound was echoed by something deeper that rumbled through Penny's body.

"Wow. Your belly really is complaining." Cisco looked around for the waitress.

"Cisco?" The sound pulsed again. "That wasn't my stomach."

Their eyes met for the briefest moment before the two friends shoved back their chairs and dashed out of the café, leaving Trevor hurrying behind.

"There!" Penny pointed at the looming giant who towered over the building from a street away. "What is it?"

"She's *enormous.*" Trevor's face was white, and a thin sheen of nervous sweat beaded on his brow.

"That's what he said." Cisco ducked Penny's absent-minded slap to the back of his head. "Fine. but who is she?"

Penny shot Trevor a sideways glance. "Anything to do with your new pet project, Trev?"

He spread his arms, eyes still glued to the meandering giant. "Not me."

The entity was a woman. A very tall woman, tall enough to tower over the buildings clustered around her. She wore a headpiece that reminded Penny of a Bollywood movie, and a green silk dress strung with jewels to match. In her hands—*all four of them*—she held weapons and a shield.

A hum buzzed near Penny's ear and she jerked away, swatting at a bee. Two more passed, and to Penny's alarm, a swarm the size of a large dog appeared around the corner to follow them.

ZzzzzzZZZZ. The bees floated away, moving toward the giant woman.

"Come, my children!" The woman's voice boomed, her accent thick. "Find the one they call Paddy. Find him and bring him to me." The buzzing intensified.

"OI!" Penny yelled as loud as she could, waving her arms to attract the attention of the giantess. "Down here!"

Big brown eyes turned her way. The nearby buzz grew louder as the swarm of bees drifted back toward her.

Uh-oh. Maybe this wasn't the amazing idea it seemed like a second ago. Penny slipped a hand behind her back, crossing her fingers and hoping her gamble would pay off instead of getting her—and probably everyone around her—killed.

"What do you want with Paddy?" Penny yelled, trying to keep her voice friendly despite the volume, and the fear that crawled up her spine as the bees lazily approached, darting to and fro in a thick cloud.

"He has summoned the gods and goddesses to discuss the future of our kind." The goddess spoke in a voice that carried across the buildings and streets, in a low, rhythmic hum. "He did not, however, explain how we were to find him. I am unfamiliar with your city, child."

"I can take you to him," Penny called. "But you need to call back your bees so they don't hurt anyone. And don't step on anything!"

The deity regarded Penny for a moment, her face still. Then, she gave a slow nod. "Be still so they may bring you to me. They will not harm you, and it will be tedious trying to navigate the city without them." She regarded Penny for a moment longer. "Perhaps this will be easier if you close your eyes."

"You got my back, Dangerino?" Penny murmured.

"Always," Cisco replied. He squeezed her hand, then stepped away. "I'll be right behind you. Behind and below. Way, way below."

Beside him, Trevor edged away. "I'm allergic to bees," he whimpered.

The bees stretched into a wide cloud, and more flitted from the sky above to fill the spaces between them, creating a thick blanket that blocked out the sun.

Penny held her breath and squeezed her eyes shut, praying she wouldn't inhale one and invoke the wrath of their goddess. She flinched when the first one landed on her face but clung to a shred of calm as more joined it. Soon, every inch of Penny's body crawled with the insects.

The bees took flight, a thunderous buzz that drowned out Penny's senses as they cradled her body, lifting her into the air. When she cracked her lips to gasp in a breath of air, they parted to allow her to breathe.

Penny rose, the sensation more like being swung around in a maggot-filled hammock than flying. She endured it for what seemed like hours, although it was only the space of twenty strained breaths. Still, the crawling sensation over her skin still beat the sudden fall when they abruptly let go.

Thwap. Penny landed on a firm, leathery surface, heart pounding. She tried to stand, but a movement made her shaking legs buckle beneath her.

"Sit, child. I do not wish to drop you."

Penny looked up into the face of the goddess whose large fingers cupped her safely.

"I am Bhramari Devi," the goddess told her. "Take me to the one named Paddy."

CHAPTER SIX

"We've got fourteen broken streetlights, nine signs, and a bicycle. How am I supposed to explain *that*?" Crenel slapped the report back on his desk and sat back in his chair, an unlit cigarette dangling from his fingers.

Penny shrugged. "I did my best to keep her out of trouble. I don't think she meant to step on all that stuff."

"You did great, kid." Crenel tapped the report with one finger. "If not for you, this all could have been a lot worse."

"We can't undo the damage that was done," Penny agreed, a small frown pressing her brow. "But I'm sure we can figure out a way to prevent it from happening again. Does the city have a property somewhere on the outskirts of town that can be used for meetings like this in the future?"

Crenel pursed his lips. "They just might. Damn. I know you're a smart kid, but you're starting to run circles around me, and it's making me feel old."

Penny laughed as she reached for the door to his office.

"That's because you *are* old." She slipped out and closed it behind her just in time to avoid a balled-up piece of paper that shot toward her head.

Penny wandered down the corridors of the Academy. Her burger had been cold by the time Cisco returned to the Academy with it, but it had filled her stomach, and now a gentle lethargy had set in.

Tuesday was her day off. Apart from her unscheduled defense class that morning, she didn't have anything else on for the day. She checked her watch. Amelia and Red should be finishing up the European mythology class right about now. Penny hurried off to meet them.

She almost tripped over Trevor, who had wandered around the corner juggling an open laptop in one hand and frantically typing with the other as he walked.

"Oh good, you made it back." Penny waited for his attention to refocus.

A slow grin grew across his face. "Penny! Wow, that was the most amazing thing I've ever seen, despite the bees. I mean, I like bees, they're good for the environment and stuff. It's the part where they can kill me that kind of freaks me out, you know?" He looked up as if expecting a giant hand to squash him for insulting the goddess's minions.

"It was pretty cool," Penny admitted. "Did you make any progress on your big case today?"

Trevor shook his head. "It was a bust. I got there too late and missed my chance."

"The goons said the arcade game will be back tomorrow." She watched him closely, hiding her smile when he jerked his head up in shock.

"What? What arcade game?" He scurried back. "I never said anything about an arcade game."

"Yeah, you did," Penny reminded him gently. "When you arrived at the cafe. I just assumed…"

"I'm so bad at this," Trevor moaned. He rubbed his face with one hand, which caused the laptop to sway as it balanced precariously on the other. "I was supposed to keep it a secret!"

"Why?" Penny darted a hand out to prop the slipping laptop up.

Trevor righted it gratefully. "It's just… You guys get to do so much cool stuff. I'm not jealous or anything — I know I couldn't do half of what you do. But when I found *Polybius* and realized what it meant…" He trailed off.

"You thought you'd found something right up your alley?" Penny still didn't know what his interest was in the game, but she didn't press him. "Look, I get it. If I stumbled on a case involving Rainbow Serpents, I'd bust my ass to get in on it, despite how underqualified I might be."

Trevor looked up hopefully. "You would?"

"Of course!" Penny replied. "But do you know what else I'd do?"

"What?" Trevor looked dubious, but let her continue.

"I'd ask my friends for help," she told him gently.

Trevor's eyes dropped to his laptop. "Yeah. Yeah, you're right." His eyes met hers. "And that's *exactly* what I'm gonna do." He whirled around on one foot and walked away.

"That's…not where I thought that was going," Penny mused. She was going to chase him, but a nearby door opened and students began filing out.

"Penny!" Amelia waved at her. "Red asked if we can help him with an assignment tonight. Are you in?"

"Sure!" Penny looked back for Trevor one more time, but he'd already disappeared in the crowd. She sighed and turned back to her friends. She would hunt him down and press for answers later. "What's the brief?"

Red's eyes gleamed. "Gold, Penny. The brief is gold!"

"I thought it was just leprechauns that got their knickers in a twist over yellow rocks," Penny commented. "But I see it's *all* Irishmen."

Red laughed. "Are you saying that you wouldn't be excited if you found a giant ingot lying on the beach?"

"Well… no. I'd probably wet myself with excitement." Penny braced herself as Red clapped her on the shoulder. Since his werewolf bite, he'd gotten a lot stronger.

"That's the spirit, lass." Red looped one arm through Penny's and another through Amelia's. "Now, we're looking for a thing called a gold-digging ant. Can you believe the wee bugger goes and digs up gold in the sand?"

"An ant? You want to find one tiny ant at a beach?"

Red laughed. "He's not tiny. Supposed to be the size of a wee dog. A proper wee dog, I mean, not those big-eared ones that look like rats."

"Red, Chihuahuas *are* proper dogs." Amelia sighed. "And you'd better get used to them because I have three at home."

Thinking back on her earlier discussion with the gigantic goddess and her bee powered flight, Penny decided that yes, she could believe in a giant ant that spent its days looking for gold. "What class is this for?" she asked, curious. It didn't sound like anything she had read about in their shared mythology classes.

"It's for geospatial and signals intelligence." Red flashed a grin. "I'll be bringing some fancy equipment along with me. All I have to do is use the equipment to find it, then catch the wee bastard on camera—and if some gold happens to fall in my pockets, the professor doesn't need to know that."

"What do you need us for?" Penny asked suspiciously. "It doesn't sound terribly difficult."

Red gave her a look of mock horror. "Out on the beach by myself? All night? I'll be so bored my kneecaps will fall off."

Penny had to laugh at that. "Fair enough. When are we going?"

"Right now," Amelia explained. "Red already has the equipment packed and ready to go. Where's Cisco? Might as well bring him too."

"He was with me before, but I got caught chatting with Crenel," Penny explained. "You wouldn't *believe* the day we've had."

Red shot off a quick text message, his phone pinging barely a minute later. He pumped a fist in the air. "My boy is in!"

"Do I need to bring anything?" Penny asked. "At the very least, Boots will want to come."

"Go get your wee snake and maybe a coat. You might have a better tan than me, but you're a downright wimp in a nice breeze."

Shaking her head but unable to disagree with him,

Penny headed back toward her room, flipping the bird over her shoulder back at Red. She arrived at her dorm room and pushed open the door. "Boots? Boots, where are you?"

The room was a mess. *Wow, I didn't realize it had gotten this bad.* She shook off the thought, resolving to spend the weekend cleaning it. "Boots?"

Penny looked up at hearing a rustle overhead. Boots' tiny face peeked out over the edge of the narrow wardrobe in the corner of the room.

"What are you doing up there?" Penny lifted her arms so that Boots could lower herself down safely. "Actually, forget *why* you're up there. How did you *get* there?"

Boots gave a frustrated hiss and wobbled her head. Her tail twitched with irritation.

"I'm sorry, my dear. I do wish I could understand you." Penny let the snake wrap around her shoulders, wincing when she squeezed tight. The serpent's behavior concerned her. Boots wasn't normally this clingy. "Are you getting sick?"

The head hovering next to her cheek shook from side to side.

"Are you hurt?"

Boots shook her head again.

"Is it… *Boy* trouble?" Steele's words were still playing on Penny's mind, though she had done a fairly good job of shoving them back to her subconscious.

Boots head-butted Penny's ear in exasperation, then shook her head for the third time.

"Then I really can't help you." Penny scratched Boots

under the chin and felt the snake relax a little. "But I have good news. We're going on a road trip!"

Boots perked up at that, happily riding on Penny's shoulders down to the car. When they got there, Red, Amelia, and Cisco were already waiting for them.

"Hurry up, slowpoke." Red turned the key in the ignition and started the Jeep.

"Is this one of Mack's?" Penny asked.

"Sure is," Red said. "He funded most of the equipment for the class."

Although Mack had told his former students they were welcome to borrow his vehicles and take them out on the racetrack any time, Penny hadn't had the chance this semester. She slid into the back seat of the pristine car with a happy sigh, nestling Boots between her and Cisco.

"Hey, Boots." Cisco reached out to stroke Boots, but she wriggled across his lap instead, shoving herself between him and the window. She nosed the button to open it and hung her head out the side.

Cisco laughed, shuffling closer to Penny to give the serpent room. "She's like a big goofy puppy dog."

Penny turned a warm smile his way. "She wants you to *think* she's like a big dopey dog. She is a cunning snake though, and twenty to one, she has no interest in staring out the window."

"Then why is she over there?" Cisco asked.

Penny giggled. "She's matchmaking."

She didn't admit it out loud, but Boots had shown signs of being well and truly sick of Penny's pining after Cisco. After their first date had gone so horribly wrong, he hadn't asked her again. Penny was beginning to think she would have to take the initiative. She wasn't normally shy about asking guys out, but things were somehow different with Cisco. She had spent all of six months trying to convince herself she wasn't interested in him and that by the time they started getting to know each other, she would be back living in Australia.

During her second semester at the Academy, she had simply been too busy. Between searching for a job and dealing with life as a hunter of myth and legend, she had no time for romance. At least, that's what she had told herself.

It's not like life is going to get any quieter, she told herself. *The rip in the veil is still tearing, and things are only going to get busier.* She took a deep breath and spoke before she could chicken out. "Are you free for an early dinner Friday night?" she asked in a low voice. "I have to be at work by eight, but I thought… You know, a date."

"No, I've got plans with me girl," Red called loudly from the front seat. He grinned over his shoulder. "Or were you asking another devastatingly handsome man?"

Amelia slapped his chest. "She wasn't asking you, idiot."

"I *know* that," Red replied with exaggerated patience. "I was being funny."

"No one laughed," Amelia pointed out dryly. Then, she turned big eyes toward the back seat. "Well? *Are* you free, Cisco?"

The object of her attention muttered something under his breath, his face as red as a gnome's pointed hat.

"What was that?" Amelia pressed.

"I said I'm busy planning a double homicide," Cisco repeated.

Penny laughed. "Oh, please, let me help. I'll bring the shotgun if you bring the shovel."

In the corner, Boots coughed a laugh.

Cisco jabbed a thumb toward Red. "Good luck digging a hole big enough for his stupid head."

"It'll be fine," Penny replied, deadpan. "As long as Amelia doesn't insist on being buried with her enormous shoe collection."

"You're damn right, I do!" Amelia shot back. "And all of my handbags, too. It'll take you months to dig a hole that big!"

"Our plan is foiled." Cisco sighed dramatically. "I guess I'm free, then."

Penny couldn't stop the excited grin from spreading across her face.

Amelia couldn't stop herself from pointing it out. "Jeez, girl. You look like a fourteen-year-old meeting her first celebrity crush." Despite their close proximity, Amelia easily dodged the shoe Penny lobbed at her head. "What? I think it's adorable."

"And about time, too." Red changed gears, slowing the car and rolling into a free spot by the side of the road. "But enough of that romantic shite. We've got work to do."

CHAPTER SEVEN

P enny was the first one out of the car. She popped the trunk and began unloading Red's equipment.

"Really?" Amelia grumbled as she dislodged an item from the trunk. "They're supposed to be training you up to use the most sophisticated equipment in the world, and they give you a dollar shop metal detector?"

"That's not theirs," Red told her. "And she wasn't from the dollar shop. Were you, my magnificent lass?" He stroked the machine in Amelia's arms. "My grandpa used to take me out hunting treasures with Bessie here. Found her at a pawn shop, cost him three whole pounds. Mack offered me some big fancy version, but I don't trust it like I trust old Bessie."

"I take it back, Penny," Amelia told Penny. "Boys are awful. All of them. You should run while you still can."

Penny chuckled. "Too late. He knows I'm interested now."

Together, they headed down to the beach. Penny squinted into the afternoon glare as they waited for Red to set up his equipment. He clicked open the large boxes and pulled out smaller ones, set up a flimsy folding chair, and threw a packet of markers on the ground.

Beside her, Cisco's eyes were locked on the horizon.

"Sorry," he murmured.

"What for?" Penny asked, confused.

His eyes flickered toward her, then back to the scenery. "Making you ask. Look, I can face down the Kraken or fight off an urban legend. When it comes to girls, though, I'm…"

"A bit of a wuss?" Penny asked, grinning.

Cisco laughed and nodded. "Yeah. That."

Penny leaned against him, welcoming the reprieve from the crisp wind. "Then it's lucky I've got enough balls for the two of us."

Cisco spluttered and began to protest but was interrupted by a call from Red.

"It's ready! Stop trying to get in each other's pants and come help."

The beach was soon dotted with tiny orange flags marking out the area that Red intended to search for the giant gold-digging ant.

Penny held the clipboard, marking off each sector as Cisco paced back and forth inside of it. The sensor he swept over the sand would penetrate the sand, showing any variations in the density below. Red's theory was that it would pick up tunnels dug by the ant, helping them to pinpoint its lair.

Nearby, Red squinted into a small tablet screen with Amelia watching over his shoulder. Penny glanced up in time to see Amelia point excitedly at the small display.

"Cisco!" Red called. "Jump on over to sector eight. No, the next one." When Cisco paused, counting off each of the squares they'd marked off, Red groaned. "Fine, sector nine. No, that's— Just take two bloody steps to your right! That's my boy."

"Hey, I can't help it if you're giving bad instructions." Regardless, Cisco swept the sensor over the area, methodically working from one end to the other.

"Stop!" Red dropped the tablet into the sand and darted for the pile of equipment beside him. A moment later, he withdrew old Bessie. He kissed the shaft and held it aloft. "Don't fail me now, love."

"I remember when he used to talk to me like that," Amelia remarked wistfully. Still, she grinned as Red ran over to where Cisco had stopped, patiently waiting.

Penny trotted over toward them. "Red, am I supposed to mark off section four? You interrupted Cisco before he finished it."

Red didn't answer, crowing with delight instead as his metal detector squealed loudly.

"All hands on deck!" Red tossed the metal detector aside and fell to his knees, pushing sand to one side with his big hands.

He had already explained that shovels were out of the question. The goal was to photograph the specimen, not to accidentally decapitate it with a poorly placed spade.

Penny dropped the clipboard and joined the small circle and helping to unearth the gold thief's lair. She jumped back when the middle of their small hole began to collapse, the center writhing and wiggling as a creature pushed two pincers up into the fresh air.

"That's… What is that?" Amelia squealed.

The appendages were huge, each one the size of Penny's hand. The rest of the ant climbed out of the fallen sand, its oversized legs decked with pretty gold chains and bracelets. It crawled over toward Penny, stopping to vomit out a mouthful of mucous-covered jewelry. Penny scurried back.

Red already had his phone out, snapping pictures of their prize. "Isn't he beautiful?"

"It vomits gold, so I suppose it can't be *that* bad." Amelia grimaced. "But I expected ingots. Where did he get all *that*?"

Red got down to his belly, trying to get a better image. "I guess ingots are in short supply on a tourist beach these days. That was probably all dropped by beachgoers, lost in the sand."

Suddenly, the ant's pincers clacked. It scurried away, kicking up loose sand into Red's face as it ran. "Hey! I wasn't finished, you wee prick."

"That thieving bastard is going for our stuff," Cisco yelled. He took off after it, Penny on his heels.

The ant, its speed seemingly increased with its size, had already reached their small pile of gear. It threw aside Penny's cardigan and snatched up her wallet, waving it in the air before diving into the sand.

"Get him!" she yelled as Cisco closed in on the half-buried insect.

Cisco dove, and so did something else. Penny watched in shock as the winged creature plucked the ant from the sand and flung it across the beach.

"What the fuck was that?" Cisco asked, spitting sand out of his mouth.

"I don't know, but that little prick still has my stuff." Penny turned on her heel, racing toward the fallen ant. The flying beast swooped again, tackling the ant and wrestling Penny's purse away from the insect. It struggled to gain height as its foe clutched at the strap.

Penny snatched at her purse, jerking it away from the strange creatures. "Dammit!" The strap dangled in two lengths, snapped in the middle. The winged Myther shot into the air, spun once, then swooped back down to dive at Penny's head. She belted it with her purse and it tumbled onto the sand.

"It's a gryphon!" Red exclaimed, appearing beside her.

"It couldn't have been," Penny said. She watched as it flapped back into the air and let out a roar. "Gryphons have a bird's head. This looks more like a reptile of some kind."

"Dragon, actually. It's a pixiu," Amelia informed them. She shrugged at the bewildered faces turned her way. "Didn't you see that chart comparing animal mixes back in Madera's classroom? It has the head of a dragon, body of a lion, and feathered bird wings. Unlike a gryphon, which is comprised of—"

"No time for a biology lesson, Amelia," Cisco panted. "But I think you're right—they're attracted to gold, too. Look." He pointed to the beast, which was now digging in the collapsed tunnel made by the gold thief.

"Shite." Red ran toward it, waving his arms and hollering as he went. "Piss off, you bugger! Piss off! I need that gold for my assignment!"

Red snatched and waved at the fluttering pixiu, but it was persistent. It roared at Red and swiped a paw at him until he backed off, then resumed its search for the gold.

A flurry of sand pelted Penny's calf as the gold-digging ant took off to protect its stash. It raced into the fray, darting in between Red's legs and tripping him before leaping into the collapsed tunnel. Sand puffed and undulated as it disappeared into the tunnels below.

"No!" Red howled as the ant disappeared into the sand. "That gold was mine, you wee feathery trollop!" He waved his fist at the pixiu, who flapped away down the beach now that the gold was gone.

"It's okay, Red." Amelia went over to help him up, dusting sand off his face before accepting a kiss from him. "I got pictures of them. Two Mythers in one! It's not gold, but you should get at least a little extra credit for it, right? And anyway, all that stuff was lost property. You would have had to hand it in to the police in case it was claimed."

Red brightened and kissed her on the cheek. "I knew I kept you around for a reason." When Amelia raised a threatening eyebrow, he backtracked. "Because you're smart. You're clever, and pretty, and wise. Most of all, you're far too good for a bastard like me."

She grinned and hugged him. "Exactly."

CHAPTER EIGHT

Penny left her class with Professor Glass the next morning feeling pretty good about herself. He had—perhaps inspired by her choice of weapons the previous day—run the class through a brush up on medieval weapons. Thanks to her recent practice, Penny had come out on top.

That good feeling had been all but sucked out of her by the end of the next lesson.

"This current influx is not ceasing. No, the pantheons of old are passing over at a higher rate. As it has always been, not all of them mean to live harmoniously with us." Hardwick slapped the board, leaving a smudge right in the middle of a long list of beings from Greek mythology that had recently been sighted.

Everything from the Hecatoncheires and Cyclopes to the Titans themselves had been seen stalking the streets of America, and other continents. Many of them had been destructive, though the loss of life had been minimal thus far.

"Why aren't the other gods doing something about it?" Kathy asked.

"Maybe they are." Penny gave the girl a comforting smile but didn't elaborate.

Her position at Paddy's meant that she had a rare insight into the many alliances and safeguards the Mythers were attempting to create in order to stem the tide of malevolent entities. Bacchus in particular was invested in making sure that the reputation of the Greek gods remained good in the public eye.

As far as Penny knew, his work to build an alliance of the gods was progressing well. They'd managed to talk down some of the more sentient new additions to the real world, and had quietly dispatched a few of the more vicious ones. All that, however, was information she had been asked to keep quiet.

A bell chimed and the class stood, eager to shake off the direness of the class and take advantage of the short break before they attended the Cybermythology lesson after lunch. It was a mandatory class, so Penny knew it would be full.

Penny rubbed her eyes as she wandered to the Academy dining hall. "Two down, two to go," she said to Amelia. "Dean March must hate us. Why else would she schedule three mythology classes in a row?"

Despite her interest, the Greek Mythology class had been a dry, factual account of the legendary myths, and a catalog of which ones had been sighted. Even the professor's warning at the end of class hadn't been enough to take the edge of boredom away.

"Food." Amelia nodded at the doorway ahead. "Food will wake us up. And coffee."

Penny and Amelia made a beeline for the dining hall. Just as Amelia shoved the door open and the aroma of warm Mexican food wafted through, Penny felt a hand on her arm. It was Trevor.

"I'll join you in half a sec, Amelia." Penny waved her friend ahead. "What's up, Trevor?"

Trevor fidgeted nervously. "I need a favor."

"Sure. What is it?" Penny waited patiently, but Trevor didn't answer until three more students had passed them.

Once they were alone, he continued, "I need you to tell Prof Anand I'm not coming to class."

"Okay," Penny answered slowly. "Am I giving her an excuse?"

His eyes brightened and he gave her a wobbly grin. "I'm *on a case.*"

"Oh. Oh!" Penny raised her hand for a high five. The palm that slapped hers was cold and sweaty. "Are you sure there's nothing else I can help with?"

Trevor shook his head resolutely. "Not yet. Once I get the go-ahead from Agent Crenel—"

"Wait." Penny waved him down. "He hasn't given you a mission code yet?"

Trevor straightened. "He's about to," he clarified. "I have a meeting with him now. *Then* I'm on the case."

Though Penny wondered if his confidence was entirely warranted, she congratulated him. "I'll let Anand know," she promised. "Are you coming in for some lunch?"

Trevor shook his head. "I have to prep my presentation."

"Presentation?" Penny wondered, but Trevor had already darted away. "I think he might be underestimating Crenel's love of brevity." The Special Agent was notorious for his loathing of wordy requests.

Brushing off the encounter, Penny hurried to join Amelia in the queue for lunch. The day's spread was a large tray of paella with corn chips, tortillas, tomato salad, grilled corn cobs, and guacamole.

Cisco was already in line when Penny arrived. He waved at her and gestured to a table where Red was sitting, a pained expression on his face.

"Oh, the poor dear is starving," Amelia teased. She flashed Penny a quick grin. "You're gonna have to help me carry his lunch back."

Since his wolfish transformation, Red's appetite had settled a little. He still ate twice as much as a normal human, though, and was prone to letting everyone around him know if a meal was running too late for his empty stomach to bear.

"Fine," Penny conceded. "But he's not getting my leftovers until I'm actually finished, okay? If I have to leave for the loo or something, you'd better guard my food with your life."

"Pinkie swear." Amelia crooked her little finger and clasped it around Penny's, giggling.

They filled plates for themselves, and Amelia happily accepted the serving platter Cook handed her for Red.

"Poor boy, he's wasting away over there." Cook looked ready to pounce over the servery to hand Red the dish herself. "You make sure you pile it up nice and high, now!"

"Yes, Cook." Amelia did as she was instructed, confident

that even with her boyfriend's voracious appetite to contend with, the kitchen would have more than enough to feed every student on the premises.

The break passed quickly, and Penny felt ready to tackle the rest of the day with a full belly and a hot coffee when she arrived at her next class.

Anand waited for the last of the straggling students to file in and take a seat before she closed the door. She glanced around, lips pursed. "Where is Trevor?"

Trevor had not only taken a deep interest in the class, but he was also Anand's go-to when she needed a class assistant. Now, his usual seat in the front corner of the classroom was empty.

"He's on a case, Professor." Penny figured there was no need to let Anand know the "case" hadn't technically been approved yet. Whatever Trevor was working on, he seemed to believe it was urgent enough to miss his favorite class.

Anand looked down over her spectacles. "*Trevor* is on a case?"

Mara frowned and raised a hand. "I didn't think our missions were allowed to impact on class attendance."

"They're not," Anand snapped. "Not without permission from their instructor."

Oh. Penny hoped she hadn't gotten either Trevor or Agent Crenel in trouble with the usually kind instructor.

Anand moved on with the class, one that covered several instances of computer viruses that defied logic, a string of incredible luck after a chain of emails was passed around, and a wizened old lady who claimed to be cured of cancer through the good people sharing her social media story. Further testing revealed the woman had no DNA. She was a Myther, complete with a convincing but false stack of papers "proving" her medical claims.

"The prevalence of these cyber myths-turned-reality is increasing," Anand told them. "And the forms they take seem to shift and change as fast as the internet itself. I cannot stress how much care you must take online or on a device whose origins you are not certain of."

She dismissed the class with one last shake of her head at Trevor's empty seat, one that stuck with Penny as she headed toward her next lesson.

British Mythology ended with a similar warning—that creatures from Myth and Legend were pouring through the Veil at an unprecedented pace. Over in England, politicians were fighting over what to do about it, with suggestions ranging from a ban on Mythological activity unless properly licensed, to a task force comprised almost entirely of Mythers themselves designed to thwart the less desirable newcomers.

Penny left the class with her head swimming, thankful that Cisco, Amelia, and Red had also been made to choose the class this semester so she could debrief.

"Do they really think they can just conscript a bunch of Mythers into an army to fight their own?" she asked, pushing around tater tots on her plate.

"They're politicians. They think they could conscript half the population to scrub their bathrooms if they needed to." Cisco offered Penny a jug of gravy, but she shook her head.

Red pushed back from the table. "It's all bollocks, anyway. They can't force them to do anything. If they tried, they'd get their asses handed back to them on a pike."

"Asses go on a platter, Red." Penny slid her still-full plate toward him, and he sat back down with a grin as he tucked into her uneaten dinner. "Heads go on a pike."

"And where do you think they'll find their heads?" Red asked through a mouthful of food.

"Good point." Penny wiped her face and eyed Cisco. She jutted her chin toward his napkin and, blushing, he wiped the smudge of grease off his chin.

"Is that my son using something other than his shirt to wipe his face?" Professor Madera walked over, placed a stack of folders on the table, and pulled out a chair, ignoring her son's groan as he shrank down in his seat.

"Come on, Mom. You promised you'd stop embarrassing me in public."

"I was complimenting you. Or perhaps whoever instigated this new Cisco." Her smile didn't entirely reach her eyes, though, and her mouth quickly puckered back into a worried line.

"Mom? What's wrong?" Cisco leaned over and placed a hand on his mother's arm.

"Nothing at all. I simply wanted to ask how you are all doing with your classes this semester." Madera's eyes flicked to Penny. "We have some new teachers, some from quite a distance away."

"Classes are fine." Cisco leaned back and rubbed his stomach. "Boring, but fine."

"My son. Learning about living, breathing, magical beings, and he calls it boring." Madera shook her head, patting Cisco's arm as she stood. "As long as 'boring' is as bad as it gets, I am happy. But if any of you are having trouble with your classes—or the professors teaching them—you come and see me, okay?"

"Classes are fine, Mom, and so are the professors. We don't have another Jones. It's not like you to worry so much." Cisco squeezed her arm. "Are you sure there's nothing wrong?"

Madera quirked an eyebrow. "Wrong? Apart from the newest intake, which is full of egotistical young men and women who are sure that the answer to the Veil's secret lies on Instagram, seventy papers that need grading, ninety-two applications for the teaching assistant's job I posted and the pile of washing *someone* left on the hallway floor this morning? Everything's fine."

Cisco winced. "Sorry. Probably should have warned you I was bringing my laundry."

"Cisco!" Penny thumped his arm. "You lazy shit! She's your mother, not your slave."

Madera chuckled. "Actually, the washing wasn't left for me to do. I recently acquired a fairy prone to doing house-work. I happened to ask Cisco if he had anything that needed doing because if she isn't kept busy, she does tend to get into mischief. Once, she baked ninety-two cupcakes in a single morning. They were hard as rocks, unfortunately." She eyed her son. "However, her tiny frame is unsuited to lifting a basket piled three feet high with clothes. I almost broke my neck when I tripped over it this morning."

Cisco stuck his tongue out at Penny, who simply rolled her eyes in response.

"The offer is open to the three of you. The fairy is quite good at removing stubborn stains, actually." Madera smiled, a twinkle in her eye. "But God help you if you leave it somewhere for me to trip over."

"Yes, Mom." Cisco stood with his mother and hugged her briefly. "Sorry."

"Don't worry yourself." Madera waited until Cisco sat down and ruffled his hair despite his grimace. "I have been used to your ways for a long time now."

Penny watched her go, wondering if the queasiness in her gut really was just the greasy dinner, or if it was trying to tell her something.

CHAPTER NINE

Penny didn't see Trevor again until late that night. She had sent him a text message after Cybermythology, warning him that Professor Anand hadn't been happy with his absence, and Trevor had replied with a rather uninformative **Thanks**.

In reply, Penny offered to buy him dinner. He accepted, as long as she didn't mind if he wasn't the best company. She texted him again.

Cisco and I will cheer you up. Meet you at Paddy's? Eight PM?

Trevor's reply was just as lackluster as his first.

Sure. See you then.

Penny itched with curiosity. Whatever was going on with those goons, the arcade machines, and Trevor's theory, she wanted to know about it. And, she had to admit to herself, she wanted to get involved.

The adventures she'd had over the past year should have scared her away. A violent poltergeist, a Kraken, a violent, bandaged serial killer. None of it had given her the very sensible idea that Mythers were dangerous.

No. Instead, working at Paddy's, mingling with Mythers, and hunting the more dangerous entities had simply given her a taste for adventure. *And whatever Trevor is up to, there's an adventure to be had.*

Cisco shoved open the door to Paddy's and stepped back to let Penny in first. She spotted Trevor immediately.

"Just a bite, little one." A slim, stunning woman leaned over him, holding out a bright, juicy apple. "It's almost as delicious as you look."

"N-no, thank you." Trevor tried to shrink down further in his seat.

"Titania!" Penny snapped. "Third strike. You're out." She thrust a finger at the door.

"What?" Titania turned big blue eyes on Penny. "I was simply offering—"

"You know the rules," Penny told her. "No feeding the humans. One month ban. If it happens again, it'll be permanent. And you know what that means?"

Titania's lower lip trembled delicately. Her eyes filled, and a glistening tear rolled down her cheek.

Penny was unmoved. She had seen this display far too many times from the local fae after breaking Paddy's rules. "One." She held a finger up.

"I'm sorry, Penny. Please, find it in your—"

"Two." A second finger joined the first. Penny let her gaze bore into the fae queen.

"Fine." Titania gathered her skirts in a huff and pranced past Penny and Cisco. "I'll find somewhere else to buy my mead."

"You do that," Penny called after her cheerfully. "See you in a month, Tats."

Penny strode over to Trevor. "Are you okay, mate?"

He nodded, cheeks flushed bright red and eyes nervously darting to the door. "Was she… Was she going to eat me?" he whispered.

Penny laughed. "Not a chance. Maybe abduct you for a night, but eating humans is forbidden by contract. You know the Fae—never break a promise."

"Oh." He sat up a little and gave Cisco a timid wave.

"What exactly happens if a fairy abducts you for a night?" Cisco asked. His eyes were still locked on the door Titania had flounced through.

Penny slapped his chest hard. "You get flayed alive when you get back —by me."

Wincing, Cisco took a seat. "Duly noted."

"Penny!" Munder ambled over. "I did see you speak to Titania. But you are not working this night?"

"Not tonight," Penny told him. "It's okay, she wouldn't have hurt Trevor. Maybe taught him a thing or two…" Penny winked, then chuckled when Trevor's cheeks flamed again. "I need to talk to Josh about getting another bouncer in, though."

Munder's top half wobbled in a nod. "Perhaps I might offer to help?"

Penny suppressed a snort. "I don't think you'd be suited to the job, Munder. You're way too nice."

Munder sighed. "Yes. That is a downfall of mine, I am afraid. No matter. I am sure Master Joshua will find a suitable candidate." He lifted wispy fingers in a tinkling wave, then wobbled his shapeless form back to the bar to ask for another glass of milk.

"He was terrifying." Trevor's eyes were wide. "Who is he?"

"The monster under the bed," Penny told him. "But a nice version."

"Oh." Trevor looked around, clearly uncomfortable.

"How about I go get us some drinks." Cisco tilted his head at Penny, and she mouthed a thank you. "What'll it be, Trevor?"

"Beer is fine." Trevor dug for some change, but Cisco waved him away. "Are you sure?"

"Yeah. Penny working here gets us half-price drinks. Or free, if Paddy is in." Cisco looked at Penny. "The usual?"

"Not whiskey. Maybe cider?" Penny waited until he had moved away before turning to Trevor. "So. Did you speak to Agent Crenel?"

Trevor slumped. "We had to do the meeting by phone. He said no."

"He said no?" Penny snapped. "You mean he wants you to wait until he gets back?"

Trevor shook his head morosely. "Nope. He said, and I quote, 'what the hell does a video game have to do with the Myther threat?' I tried to explain the history of the myth, but he didn't seem interested."

"Ah." Penny would have bet her life savings that the brisk dismissal was due to a combination of Crenel's technophobia and Trevor's overly detailed explanation.

Trevor let out a frustrated hiss. "This isn't some stupid idea. I know something is going on here, but I can't look into it without using the Academy resources."

"I'll talk to him." Penny grinned. "You just need to know how to handle him, that's all. You'll have to do something for me, though."

Trevor looked up, doubt etched on his face. "What's that?"

"You have to tell me *everything.*"

Crenel slapped a hand on his desk, making all three students jump. "I thought I already told you no?"

Penny guessed he was in a bad mood—it didn't take a genius for that. She was used to Crenel's temper, but Trevor looked like he wanted to hide behind the curtains.

She almost regretted dragging Trevor and Cisco along with her. However, business was business. Crenel's adamant refusal to consider Trevor's plan only made Penny more determined. And, despite Trevor's clear discomfort, this was *his* case.

"That was yesterday. Now you're gonna tell him yes." Penny grinned confidently at Trevor, who looked as forlorn as if he'd just been given a prison sentence.

Crenel tsked. "What the hell gives you that idea? I'm not wasting good resources on a goddamn computer game."

"It's not a game, Crenel," Penny told him gently. "It's an urban legend. You know, one of these things we're training to investigate? One involving secret government conspiracies and mysterious technology. I know Trevor's explanation was a bit confusing, but I think—"

"Go find something that's an actual myth," Crenel grumbled. "Then we'll talk."

"Why are you being so stubborn?" Penny snapped. Her patience was wearing thin. "I know you think technology is out to get you, but this is ridiculous!"

"I never said that!" Crenel denied. "But look around you. What the hell does an arcade game have in common with Greek gods and ancient ghosts? This is too modern. It's probably some video game company doing one of those infection campaigns."

"You mean viral," Trevor corrected. Before the words were even out, he looked like he regretted saying them.

"It's too *modern?*" Penny smirked. *I've got him now.* "So, the latest cluster of Mythers based on 'like for a cure' stories are what, Mayan legends? And the UFOs that keep appearing in Nevada are from the early 1200s?" Crenel tried to cut her off, but Penny kept going. "What about the ATM that spontaneously started calling the police every time someone used a palindromic PIN? I guess that one originated in ancient Egypt, huh?"

Crenel finally sputtered to a halt. "But he's not even a field student."

Penny didn't miss a beat. "Which is why I've agreed to lend my expertise and act as his consultant."

"You have?" Trevor whispered.

Penny nodded. "So has Cisco. With the two of us involved, how can it go wrong?"

"Are you trying to convince me or turn me off the idea?" Crenel grumbled. He hesitated, and Penny held her breath. "Fine. I'll send the paperwork over tonight."

Penny silently fist-pumped the air. She quickly sobered and said in her most professional tone, "Why, thank you,

Special Agent Crenel. We will be sure to keep you updated on the progress of our case."

She left the office quickly, tugging Cisco and Trevor along by their elbows.

Silence reigned for a moment after she closed the door carefully behind them, then Cisco let out a victory holler. "You did it!"

"*I heard that!*" Crenel's holler from the other side of the door sent them tripping down the hall, laughing.

Trevor couldn't wipe the grin off his face. "Thank you, Penny! Thank you so much!"

After high fives were passed around, Trevor slung his messenger bag over one shoulder. He hadn't ended up needing any of the meticulous notes or thick folders stuffed inside. "I need to go and get started," he told them excitedly.

Penny grabbed his wrist. "You heard what I said. Cisco and I are your consultants on this case. I don't want you running into anything dangerous without talking to us first, okay?"

Chagrined, he nodded. "Okay. I promise. I'm not doing this alone, though."

"Oh?" Trevor hadn't mentioned working on his project with anyone else. "Who?"

"I, uh, can't tell you?" Trevor hurriedly shoved his books away and backed toward the door. "My source likes to stay anonymous."

He scurried away without another word. Penny raised bewildered eyes to Cisco. "An anonymous source? Is he for real?"

"Give him a break," Cisco insisted. "It's his first case.

He's got us watching his back. Like you said, what could go wrong?"

―――――――

Penny mulled over Trevor's case and his anonymous friend the next morning during Legal and continued thinking about it while she spent the next two sessions cleaning the dorm room she shared with Amelia. Boots lounged on the bed as Penny tossed piles of clothes on top of her, wriggling to the top and pinning items down as Penny attempted to hang them in the tiny closet.

Penny dug a shirt out from beneath the serpent. "Boots, you're not making this easy, you know."

Boots simply wriggled into a new, more comfortable position.

Penny grunted in frustration, flicking a pair of pajama pants at the snake. "Seriously, do you want to live in squalor?"

Boots rolled over. The movement took her off the edge of the growing pile, and before she could halt her momentum, she had tumbled onto the carpeted floor in a twisted, writhing lump. She gave an angry hiss but tolerated Penny's giggling attempts to help her to right herself.

With Boots untangled and sulking in a neat coil in the corner, Penny quickly finished the job she had set out to do.

Penny grinned when the room was finally pristine. Her clothes were neatly organized, and her serpentine friend was finally coming out of her sulk. "Beautiful." She flopped on the bed, then groaned loudly when she checked her watch. "Bah!" She shot to her feet, grabbed a bag, and waved a finger at Boots. "I'm late for Aussie Myth class. Are you coming?"

Boots just wriggled into a more comfortable position.

"Fine. Stay behind, lazybones." Boots bared her fangs and gave an angry hiss, though Penny wasn't sure if it was due to the insult, or her orders to stay behind. "Sorry, dear. I really do have to run, though."

When Penny arrived at her class, hair a mess and face flushed from the short dash down a flight of stairs and to the other side of the Academy, Professor Steele was waiting patiently.

"Glad to see you came, Penny." She looked around expectantly before a look of dismay crept over her face. "No Boots today?"

Penny shook her head. "She's resting up. We had a big morning."

"I'm glad you made it, then. I was worried that the lack of fellow students might have turned you off the class." Steele opened a textbook and handed it to Penny. "Today, we're going to focus on the Maori creation myth, beginning with Rangi and Papa—Father Sky and Mother Earth."

Throughout the lesson, Steele occasionally stopped, staring out the window or at Penny with distracted eyes. A moment later, she would blink and return to her lecture on New Zealand and Polynesian mythology.

She wrapped up the lesson early, citing the low class number as the reason. "I structured the curriculum to allow for a bit of chatter amongst the class, you see. If there is something you'd like to cover in the extra time, we can?" She left the probing statement hanging.

Penny squirmed. She felt impelled to ask a question—any question. But her brain was still exhausted from the previous day's ceaseless lectures. "I can't think of anything in particular," she admitted.

"Perhaps we could discuss Boots, then?" Steele asked. "There are some wonderful facilities that examine Mythological beings in a safe and—"

"No, thank you." Penny shut the line of questioning down quickly. "Boots chose to follow me here. I'm not going to put her in a *facility*." The word tasted sour in her mouth.

"Oh, it's not like they lock their subjects in cages and poke them with sticks," Steele chided. "It's a wonderful setup, one that mimics their natural habitat and provides all kinds of mental stimulation. And besides, I wasn't suggesting Boots needs to go to one. I was just lamenting the chance to really examine her. Information on the species hasn't been easy to come by, you see."

"The Academy files list at least a dozen new Serpents appearing in recent months," Penny snapped. "I'm sure the information will become easier to get." *Just not from* my *friend*, she added silently.

Steele still seemed dissatisfied. "It's just a pity that none seem to display the intelligence your Boots does," she pressed. "Though perhaps they will with time and teaching."

Penny hefted her bag, ready to go. "Goodbye, Professor."

Steele passed Penny a textbook. "Here. Do some reading on what we discussed in class today. Focus on the sections about the importance of genealogy and the link between traditions and myth."

Penny clutched the fat book under one arm since her bag was already full. She headed for the door without looking back.

CHAPTER TEN

Penny arrived back in her dorm to the smell of warm madras and aromatic garlic. She cracked the door open and sniffed deeply.

"Penny!" Amelia beckoned her inside. "Thank god you're back. We were robbed!" Amelia's eyes were wide and glittered with mischief. "Someone came in and stole all our mess! Then they left a bunch of clothes in our closet, stuff I haven't seen in *forever*."

Penny laughed. "You're such a knob. Why can I smell curry?"

Amelia nodded at the covered tray on the tiny side table, then pointed at Boots, who was loosely curled into a pile on the bed. She looked to be asleep, but Penny caught the serpent watching her from between two loops of her coil. "I caught her trying to snatch a tray from the dining hall. I have no idea how she thought she was going to get it up the stairs, but damned if she wasn't trying."

"For me?" Penny sat on the bed and wrapped her arms around the reluctant snake. "You're wonderful, Boots."

Boots relaxed a little, popping her head up and nodding as if to say "yes, I know."

"I take it you missed dinner because of your cleaning spree?" Amelia asked.

Penny nodded. "I completely lost track of time and had to run to Aus-Myth. I'm bushed!" She lifted off the tray cover and inhaled again. "Mmm. Smells amazing."

"Tastes good, too." Amelia sprawled back on her bed. "You eat, I'll talk."

Penny reveled in the mild spice of the curry as she dipped shreds of garlic naan into the sauce while Amelia told her of Red's excellent grade for the assignment they had helped with. He'd been outdone only by Trevor, who had handed his assessment in three days early.

"Wait up. Trevor said he's spent every spare second on this case of his. He still managed to hand in an assignment three days early?" Penny asked between mouthfuls.

Amelia nodded wryly. "He makes it seem so easy. I can't say I'm not jealous."

Penny shrugged. "Maybe now that he has his own mission, it'll give us normal people a chance to catch up. Hey, you haven't seen him hanging around anyone in particular lately, have you?" She gave Amelia a brief explanation of Trevor's secret accomplice.

"Not really," Amelia told her. "But it's Trevor. How do you know it's even someone from the Academy? It's probably one of his gamer friends."

"That makes sense." Penny almost wished it didn't. Though she respected her friend's privacy, she didn't like getting involved in a case where one party wasn't willing to come forward. She resolved to talk to Trevor about it again. "Never mind that. Tell me what on earth I should wear on my date tomorrow night."

"I agreed to the black dress *before* I spoke to Cisco. He said to dress casual." Penny tossed the sparkling black cocktail dress back at Amelia. "That? That's not casual."

"Cisco would wear a t-shirt and jeans to visit the queen," Amelia pointed out. "Do you really trust his opinion on dress codes?"

"Well, no." Penny prickled with indecision. "Boots? What do you think?"

Boots gave an excited shiver. She'd been watching the exchange between Penny and Amelia, swaying back and forth between them. It seemed she was getting right into the spirit of dressing Penny for her date. Now, she slipped to the floor and slithered to the open closet. Boots disappeared inside, burying herself in dresses and coats.

A moment later, a green pantsuit landed on the floor. Penny and Amelia looked at each other. "That's perfect!" they cried in unison.

Penny snatched the pantsuit up, laughing at their agreement. "Boots, you're the *best!*"

Boots chuckled in agreement. She emerged from the wardrobe, one grey satin flat hooked on her tail. She dropped it at Penny's feet.

"Oh, you even picked shoes to match!" Penny kissed the serpent's head. "Classy enough for dinner, but comfortable enough if he's made other plans. Perfect!"

Penny wriggled into her outfit and slipped on the shoe

Boots had provided. Amelia searched for the other while Penny dug through her makeup case. By the time the errant shoe was uncovered, Penny was almost ready to go.

"Wow. You look hot!" Amelia presented Penny with the missing shoe. "Totes bangable."

Penny choked. "*What* did you just say?" She tried to wave away tears of laughter before they ruined her mascara.

"You heard exactly what I said." Amelia passed Penny a tissue. "And just so you know, Red and I are out for the night. *All* night."

Gasping for breath, Penny fell back onto the bed.

"No! You'll ruin your hair." Amelia hauled Penny up and put on her most innocent face. "I promise I'll behave. Mostly."

Amelia patted Penny down and inspected her hair for any damage, fussing over her until Penny finally grabbed her hands.

"Stop!" Penny smoothed her outfit. "I swear, it feels like you're more invested in this relationship than Cisco and I are."

Amelia leaned in for a hug, careful not to crease Penny's clothes. "I'm just so happy," she murmured. "Red means everything to me, and so do you guys. I want you both to be as happy as we are."

An unexpected sting prickled Penny's eyes. "Stop," she insisted. "You're gonna make me cry."

Amelia patted Penny's shoulders and spun her toward the door. "Go on. He'll be waiting for you."

"I was supposed to meet him out front five minutes

ago," Penny pointed out as she was hustled out of their room. "He won't show for *at least* another ten."

"You never know. He might surprise you!"

Taking the advice on board, Penny hurried downstairs. Cisco had insisted she meet him on the front steps of the Academy. When the soft purr of a car crept closer, she saw why.

Cisco waved out of the window as he pulled the Maserati to a stop at the bottom of the steps. "You're late," he chided.

Penny waited for him to come around and open her door. He did so with a flourish, bowing as she stepped past him to sink back into the luxurious upholstery.

"Sorry. I thought you meant five o'clock Cisco time." Penny grinned as he slid back into the driver's seat. "This is the first time ever you haven't been late."

"Me? Late?" He winked. "Maybe you've turned over a new Cisco."

"Maybe." Penny ran a hand over the leather interior. "Mack loaned you his car?"

"Mack?" The corners of Cisco's mouth turned up in a smirk. "This baby's all mine."

Penny lifted a skeptical eyebrow. "Uh-huh."

Relaxing, Cisco started the engine again. "Fine. But Mack said I was allowed to say it's mine. Just for tonight."

The car pulled away from the Academy, and Penny couldn't help a shiver of excitement. "Will you tell me where we're going yet?" she asked. "I know you said to wear something casual, but I feel underdressed for the car, let alone what comes next!"

"You look amazing," Cisco reassured her. "Don't worry.

You really don't need to dress up where we're going." He hesitated, frowning. "Although… You're not wearing heels, are you?"

Penny shook her head. "You know I hate them."

"Good." Cisco pressed a small screen on the dash and the dulcet tones of Elton John filled the car. "You don't mind if we get a bit retro tonight?"

"Not at all." Penny tried not to read too much into his song choice—*You Are So Beautiful.*

She let her eyes drift to the bright city lights as they cruised through Portland. Even the most familiar streets seemed to hold a special quality when viewed through the tinted windows, with the smooth music in the background and Cisco next to her.

She slid her gaze to him. He was focused on the road, his posture relaxed. The collar of his salmon-pink shirt was loose. His skin glistened with moisture, and his hair was still damp from the shower.

Penny looked away, a flush creeping up her face. Outside, the sun threw glittering orange sparkles across the surface of the Willamette river as they zipped along beside it.

"The river looks beautiful in the sunset," Penny said, desperate to break the silence.

"Oh, you just wait." Cisco didn't elaborate on his cryptic remark, but it seemed she would find out soon enough. He slid the car into a parking spot by the river. "Almost there."

"Almost?" Penny itched to ask questions, but he was clearly enjoying the surprise. "Okay, then. Where to?"

Cisco darted around to open her car door, then offered a hand to help her out.

Penny took it gladly, grateful she had worn sensible shoes. Getting out of the deep, comfortable seats of the Maserati may have been difficult otherwise, although she had no doubt someone like Amelia could have handled it with ease.

After a quick glance in either direction, Cisco tugged Penny's hand and led her across the street.

There goes that theory, Penny thought as he led her away from the river.

The Mexican restaurant was crowded and noisy. Cheerful voices drowned each other out, greetings called out across tables as patrons arrived and servers recognized their guests.

"Cisco!" A tall man, thin and stately, spread his arms wide. "Your table awaits, as requested. I take it this is the young lady your mother tells me you're so fond of?"

Cisco coughed. "Please, Dad. Not tonight?"

Mr. Madera smiled, and Penny was struck by his resemblance to his son. Both had grins that reached their eyes, sparkling in a way that was utterly contagious. Penny couldn't help but be charmed when he took her hand and bowed low.

"Of course, Francisco. Your table awaits." He stepped back and Cisco all but dragged Penny past the cacophony of the restaurant, toward a set of narrow stairs.

"This way." He led her up past the second floor and opened the door to their destination.

The restaurant rooftop glowed with tiny lights strung overhead. Beyond, the city lights sparkled to life one by one as the sky faded from orange to purple, the change reflecting on the rippled surface of the river. Cisco drew his phone out and tapped the screen before slipping it away. Music drifted from a nearby speaker.

Penny eyed the single table draped with a red cloth, two candles flickering in the center beside a carafe of water and two glasses. Unable to find her voice, she allowed Cisco to tug her closer, then draw her seat out.

Once he was done, he sat across from her. Worry darkened his features. "Do you like it?" he asked nervously.

Penny giggled. "It's *incredible*. Cisco, I never knew you were such a romantic!"

"It runs in the family." Cisco winked, then poured her a glass of water.

Penny gulped it down, trying unsuccessfully to settle the butterflies in her stomach. "Do I get to meet your dad later?"

Cisco groaned. "I knew you'd ask that. You can, but only if you make me a promise."

Penny nodded. "What?"

"Whatever lame, embarrassing story he comes up with about my childhood, you can't tell anyone." He leaned closer. "Swear it on your life."

"I swear." Penny grinned. "Maybe one day you can Skype my parents and learn all my childhood secrets."

"I'd love that," he replied, his easy grin reappearing.

The rooftop door scraped open and a head popped through. "You ready, Cisco?"

"Sure." Cisco quickly nudged the glasses to one side to make room for the tray laden with small plates of food. He helped the waiter set them on the table, each one holding a different dish.

Penny eyed the small yellow balls topped with salsa. "These look safe," she commented dryly.

"Don't worry," Cisco told her, grinning. "I told them you're from the land of no spice. They went easy on the chili and jalapenos."

"Hey, Australia has spice!" Penny protested. "I just don't eat any of it."

Cisco pushed the plate she'd chosen toward her. "It's a polenta stack. Go on, you'll love it. I promise."

She did, indeed, love it. The warm polenta and cool, crisp tomato were simple but expertly combined.

Cisco leaned in and scooped a little on his fork. "I just asked for a whole bunch of tasting plates. I hope that's okay? I figured that way, if you don't like something, there's plenty of other things to choose from."

Penny eyed the dozen small plates. "There's no way we can eat all of this."

Cisco laughed. "Wanna bet?"

"Okay, *you* probably could." Penny sipped her water. She looked up when the door opened again.

"Almost forgot." Cisco's father brandished a bottle of wine and two glasses. He set them on the table and bowed low. "Can't have our guests of honor getting thirsty, can we?"

"Forgot my ass," Cisco mumbled.

Penny stifled a giggle at that. "Thank you, Mr. Madera."

The man's eyes opened wide. "How did you know my name?" he gasped, one hand to his chest in shock.

"Uh…" Penny looked at Cisco.

"Ignore him," he told her. "He's the king of dad jokes."

"It is a crown I wear with pride." Mr. Madera bowed

again, then snatched up a plate from the tray and held it out to Penny. "Go on, eat. You do not want the fish to go cold."

Penny took the plate he offered and set it before her. She took a tentative bite of the spiced fish, then closed her eyes in delight. "Oh, *wow*. This is what I've been missing all my life?"

"I told you I'd convert you," Cisco announced proudly. He shooed his father away. "Off with you, old man. You're cramping our style."

"Fine, fine!" Madera backed away, then scooted back. "You know, I remember my own father trying to insert himself into my dates with your mother. 'Franco,' he would say, 'this woman is—"

"Dad!" Cisco hissed. "Go already. Please?"

"Fine." Mr. Madera spun on a heel and headed for the door. "Yell if you need anything!"

"Go!" Cisco threw his hands in the air when they were finally alone again. "I knew this was a terrible idea."

"It wasn't." Penny leaned over to touch her fingers against his. "Your dad is hilarious, I love him already."

"I didn't bring you here to fall for my dad," Cisco teased. "But we're almost out of time. Eat!" He scooped up a bite of shredded chicken into a torn-off piece of tortilla, dipped it into a sauce on the side of the plate, and held it out for Penny.

She opened her mouth and tried to bite it, but his hand wavered at the last moment. The dressing smooshed her nose.

"Oh. Oh, wow, I'm so sorry." Cisco snatched up a napkin and held it out. He managed to keep his expression of concern for a good three seconds before bursting into laughter.

Penny laughed with him, and the rest of their meal was eaten in between childhood stories, teasing, and laughter. Occasionally Cisco would reach out and rub a thumb over Penny's wrist, or she would inch her fingers close enough to link with his.

The wine had warmed Penny's cheeks. She leaned back in her seat to wave her hands at her face. "It's warm up here."

Cisco nodded, but before he spoke, his eyes brightened. "The sun is almost down. It's time!" He stood and took Penny's hand. She followed him, gripping his fingers tightly when he urged her over the edge of the building and down onto the tiny landing of a fire escape.

Penny sat on the blanket that had already been laid on the platform and dangled her legs over the edge. When Cisco was settled next to her, she moved closer to him.

He reached out to point at the river. The water was dark now that night had fallen. "Look."

Penny's eyes ran over the Willamette river, wondering what she was supposed to be looking at. The river was beautiful, true, but his insistence suggested there was something else...

A flash of blue light sparkled in the depths. "What... Oh. Oh!" Penny's breath caught as the flash of blue became a mass of sparkles. The tiny flashes darted back and forth, leaving streaks of gentle light behind them. One sprang out of the water, sailing through the air before diving under again.

"They're beautiful," Penny whispered, afraid she would break the spell. "What are they?"

"Sprites." Cisco wasn't watching the river. Instead, his gaze was locked on Penny. One arm slid around her waist and when she leaned against him, she felt him give a satisfied sigh. "I'm probably going to owe Paddy my soul for eternity for organizing it—"

"*You* organized it?" Penny asked.

"Uh…" Cisco pulled back to look at her. "That's a good thing, isn't it? Because if not, I had *nothing* to do with it."

Penny kissed his cheek. "I'd have been happy with pizza and a movie. This? This is…*wow*."

Cisco blushed, dipping his head and grinning. "Oh. Good. I hoped you'd like it."

Penny pulled his face to hers. This time when she kissed him, it was on his lips. "I love it."

CHAPTER ELEVEN

The next few days passed in a whirl. Despite Amelia's complaint that she hadn't "put the empty dorm room to good use," Penny was grateful to see her friend had stepped back a little from teasing Penny and Cisco about their burgeoning relationship.

Classes zoomed by. Penny drowned in a sea of homework, assignments, and projects. Glass had warned his class that their marks for the semester would take into account their fitness levels, so she had been spending more time at the Academy gym. With three mythology projects assigned and her shifts at Paddy's bar, though, that didn't leave much time for socializing outside of class.

It wasn't until Professor Anand commented about Trevor's second absence that Penny realized he hadn't spoken to her about his case. *Come to think of it, I haven't even bumped into him this week.* She resolved to hunt him down by the weekend to see how he was progressing.

The only blip in her week other than Trevor's absence

was her class with Professor Steele. Yet again, the professor suggested Boots would be happier if she had the chance to return home.

"Boots, do you want to go home?" Penny asked the serpent directly.

Boots shook her head emphatically.

"See?" Penny told the Professor. "She *wants* to be here. I didn't make her come with me. I didn't even think it was a possibility. She chose to do that all by herself."

Professor Steele softened. "I'm not saying you coerced her into coming. Just that, if the two of you had formed a bond, it may have caused Boots to make a decision based on *your* best interests, not hers."

"I've lived with Boots for almost three years now." Penny glared at the professor, unwilling to let her accusations stand. "I think I know her well enough to say she's happy here. Thriving, even."

"That may be the case, but your home country has a claim on her too." Steele began to pack the textbooks away. One fell to the ground, scattering a bundle of papers that had been tucked under the front cover. Steele cursed and began to pick them up.

Boots slithered over and nudged the papers closer to the professor with her tail.

"Leave those alone." Steele snatched them away, making Boots jump back in surprise.

"Come here, Boots." Penny loosened the top of her backpack, and Boots made a beeline for the safety of her regular hiding spot. Penny stood and slung it over her shoulder, then turned to the professor. "*No one* has a claim on Boots. She's her own person, and she can go where she damn well pleases."

"Of course." The odd calmness in Steele's voice belied her earlier actions. "I didn't say otherwise, dear.

"What does she expect you to do?" Amelia threw a shoe at the wall in frustration. "Force Boots into a cage, shove her on a boat, and deport her?"

Penny flopped back onto her bed. "Maybe? I don't know. Maybe I'm just blowing it all out of proportion. Now I've slept on it, it doesn't seem so bad."

"Something is up with her." Amelia jabbed a finger at Penny. "You listen to your gut, girl. It's never led you astray before."

A knock at the door interrupted their conversation. Boots raised her head and gave a happy hiss.

"Oh, shit!" Penny glanced at her watch, knowing even before she did that she was late. "I bet that's Cisco. I told him I'd catch up with him in an hour. That was an hour and a half ago!"

Cisco's voice was muffled through the closed door. "Are you decent?"

Penny scrambled to tear off her pajama top. Snatching a clean shirt from the cupboard, she glared at Boots, whose tail was surreptitiously reaching for the door handle. "I swear to God, you cheeky lizard. If you open that door before I'm dressed..."

She didn't have to finish the threat for it to be effective. Boots dropped her tail and wiggled impatiently. As soon as

Penny nodded, she pulled it open and threw herself out and wrapped around Cisco's legs.

"Woah, there, Boots." Cisco leaned down to pat her. "Someone's in a good mood today."

Penny gave him a dry look. "You've got coffee in your pocket again, don't you?"

"Coffee?" Amelia looked from Penny to Cisco, face scrunched up in confusion. "How do you hide coffee in a *pocket?*"

Grinning sheepishly, Cisco pulled out a bag of chocolate-coated coffee beans. He dangled it over Boot's head as he asked Penny if he could give some to the serpent.

"You're not leaving me much choice, are you?" Penny sighed and gave him a nod.

Boots frolicked happily for a moment, then opened her jaws wide so he could drop one in.

"Girl, you better put a stop to that before you have kids." Amelia shrugged off the look of horror Penny shot her way. She waved her hands, shooing them out. "Go! Go serenade each other against a backdrop of water nymphs or whatever it is you two do when you're together these days." Once she'd hustled them all out, she shut the door firmly behind them then yanked it back open. "If you love me, bring me home a coffee."

This time when the door thudded shut, it stayed closed.

Cisco waited for Boots to climb onto his shoulders before setting off down the hall. "Did they make any progress last night?"

Amelia and Red had spent the previous night's full moon sequestered in one of the safety rooms beneath the Academy. The sprawling labyrinth below had even escaped Cisco's knowledge of the building but had been judged by the dean to be the perfect place to study Red's changes.

Every month, Red, Dean March, Agent Crenel, and a squad of FBI researchers—and Trevor, who was in training to join them—had gathered in the dungeon-like rooms to watch and observe.

When Amelia had insisted on going with them, Penny had worried at first. Not for her safety, Red had already shown he was capable of coherent thought in wolf form by the second change—but for her relationship. Seeing her boyfriend sprout fur and claws had shaken Amelia the first couple of times, but now, several months later, she'd grown rather accepting of his condition.

"They made a new discovery last night," Penny informed him. She knew Cisco wouldn't have heard yet as Red normally spent the day after the full moon gorging on food in between naps.

"Oh?" Cisco pushed the Academy door open and they stepped into the morning sunlight together. "A cure?"

"No." Penny held back a bubble of laughter. "Apparently, Amelia has some kind of connection with him in wolf form."

"How so?" Cisco frowned.

"Every time she says the word 'sit,' his ass drops to the floor like a ton of bricks." Penny let the giggles loose. "She said he was getting so furious, but she just kept telling him to do stuff. He'd be sniffing, scratching, anything. He'd just *do* it."

Cisco chuckled at his friend's plight. "Oh man, Crenel would have loved to have been there to see that!"

"He wasn't?" Penny asked. Amelia had only mentioned that Trevor wasn't there.

"He was called away to see his mom." Cisco's voice dropped to a soft note. "My mom said it sounded urgent."

"Oh." Penny's heart sank. She hated the thought of Crenel having to deal with personal grief.

"Oh. Did Amelia mention if Trevor was there?" Cisco's sudden change of topic was accompanied by a hint of concern in his voice. "I haven't seen him around for days."

"He wasn't." Penny resolved to hunt the missing genius down by nightfall. "But maybe Tony's seen him? He might have gone into the cafe to check out that game again."

When they arrived, the coffee shop was a little busier than usual. Violet had a line five people deep, and Tony was frantically pushing out lattes and cappuccinos, though he took the time to give Penny and Cisco a quick grin.

"The usual, guys?" he called. "On the house. You might have to wait a bit, though."

"Sure." Penny gave him a distracted wave, heading over to the arcade machine. The machine itself looked identical to the one taken away, right down to the glowing "Polybius" sign across the top. However, instead of the pixelated spaceship, the screen now showed imagery of a small ball hopping over obstacles toward a gaping doorway at the end of the platform.

"Damn," Cisco cursed. "I like space shooters. I really suck at platformers." He plucked a coin from his pocket and stepped forward but stopped when Penny grabbed his arm.

"Seriously?" she asked. "You know Trevor thinks these things are dangerous."

Penny watched until the end of the demo game. She wanted to see if Trevor had been in and played it again. She watched as the bouncing ball jumped over a row of spikes, onto a moving platform over a wide chasm, then toward the ledge on the other side. The ball missed, plummeting into oblivion.

Blip, blip, beeeep. The simplistic tune of the eighties-style arcade game signaled the imaginary player's demise and the screen flicked to darkness. A peppy tune struck up as the credits began to roll.

1. pennyits trevor ... 92,012
2. ithinkifoundthem ... 77,369
3. dontworry but ... 72,568
3. ifimnotback in3wks ... 62,751
4. send help ... 62, 461
5. Maximillian Bucks ... 50,000
6. Space Invader ... 42,000
7. Win Ner ... 40,000
8. Gr8 Gamer ... 30,000

Penny's stomach dropped. "Did you *see* that?" she whispered to Cisco.

"Yeah," he managed, his voice hoarse. "That is the biggest cake I've ever seen!"

She turned to him in disbelief. "*Cisco!*"

He blinked at the urgency in her voice. "What? That's what you were talking about, right?"

Penny had her phone out before he'd finished speaking. She pulled up Crenel's name and pressed dial, then cursed as it bumped directly to voicemail. "Fuck!" She gave Cisco a very quick explanation of what she'd seen. "What a goddamn time for Crenel to be away!" She knew that whatever the agent was going through personally, Trevor's safety would be his priority

"He said 'don't worry,'" Cisco pointed out. "Maybe we should just hang back a bit, let him handle it."

"Cisco?" Penny waited for the penny to drop. It didn't. "This is Trevor. Not Red, or Clive, or Jason. *Trevor.*"

"Oh. Right." Cisco grabbed his own phone. "I'll try Dean March," he offered.

Call me. Super urgent emergency. Penny tapped send on the text message to Crenel, then clicked through to her camera. When the credits rolled again, she snapped a picture. "Let's get back to the Academy," she suggested when Cisco had rattled off a voice message to the dean. "He said *someone* was working with him. We need to find out who."

Cisco didn't falter. He ended one call and began another. "Mom? Yeah, look, we've got a bit of a situation. No, we need Agent Crenel, but he's not answering, and neither is Dean—" he stopped to listen a moment. "Oh. Damn. No, we can handle it. Thanks, Mom. You too."

Penny didn't wait until his phone was away before asking what Madera had told him. "What did she say?"

Cisco grimaced. "Before they left, they asked not to be contacted. Guess we're on our own."

Penny sighed. "Then we'd better come up with a plan. We said we'd be here for Trevor if he needed us. Well, now he does." She was headed out the door of the coffee shop when her phone rang. Despite her confidence just moments ago, she was relieved he had called back so fast. "Thank God."

"Penny? What's wrong?" The agent's voice was terse

and Penny was hit with guilt for interrupting him at such a sensitive time.

"Agent Crenel? I'm so sorry. Is your mother okay?" *If he says no, maybe he can put me in touch with DeLouise,* she decided. Though Trevor had said he was fine, she wasn't about to risk the life of her friend, even if he'd be embarrassed if it turned out she'd called in the entire bureau as backup for nothing.

"Well, she's close to the end. Just a few minutes to go, but that's fine. We've planned a quick celebration for afterward, just tacos and a few drinks. Nothing that can't be interrupted." Crenel covered the phone, but it didn't quite muffle his voice. "Not now, damn it. I'm on a call. Yes, I know she's close, but is it really the end of the world if I miss it?"

"Uh, should I call back in a few?" she asked, thrown by Crenel's talk of celebrating his mother's demise. The agent's brisk demeanor in the face of apparent tragedy was unexpected, to say the least. "I mean, I'm really, really sorry about your mum, but—"

"Sorry?" Crenel barked. "What for?"

Geez, he really didn't like his mum, did he? "Look," Penny gave up, her urgency over Trevor overriding her concern for the agent's apparently unaffected feelings. "I know this is a terrible time for it, but I just found a really cryptic message Trevor left behind. It sounds like he's in danger, Crenel, and he needs our help."

"I'll leave right now." He snapped something else, but this time covered the phone well enough that Penny couldn't make it out. "Jessica and I are two and a half hours away. I'll call you back as soon as we're in the car."

Rather than walk back to the Academy, Cisco called a cab, letting Penny grill the staff while he waited outside to flag it down.

"Three or four days?" Penny groaned. "You can't be any more specific than that?"

Tony shook his head slowly, then froze. "Wait. Maybe I can. Violet, wasn't he playing that game when those weirdos in suits came to swap the change box over?" He turned to Penny. "They come in on Wednesdays."

Violet pursed her lips, thinking. Then her eyes lit up. "That's right! He left just after them. He hadn't even touched his quarter-shot-soy-caramel-frappucino."

Tony stared at her. "You remember that god-awful chain of coffee combinations, but not what day it was?"

Violet shrugged, the dishcloth squeaking as she rubbed the inside of a glass. "I'm a barista, Tony. Not a walking calendar."

Once Penny was sure they couldn't offer any more information, she left to wait with Cisco. "Tony said he'll email us the security footage from the last few days, but he and Violet are pretty sure he hasn't been in since Wednesday."

Crenel phoned back just as they pulled into the parking lot of the old building.

"Tell me everything you have," Crenel barked, not bothering to say hello.

"All I know is that Trevor is missing," Penny told him quickly. "The only lead we have is a badly-coded message left on the high scoreboard of an arcade game."

"What? Dammit, I should have listened to the boy."

Crenel paused. Then, quieter, "If you say I told you so, Jessica, I swear to *God...*"

"Crenel?" Penny pulled the agent's attention back to their conversation. "Look, the message said he had a lead. He told us not to worry for a couple of weeks, but that's ridiculous. I mean, it's *Trevor.*"

"I get your meaning, don't worry." Crenel hissed air through his teeth. "Fool boy. He should have kept you in the loop."

"That's our fault, too," Penny protested. "He's never worked a real case before, not in the field. We should have been checking in more frequently."

"Didn't he say something about outside help?" Crenel asked. "Let's chase that person down. They might know what lead he was chasing."

Penny's heart fell. She had assumed the agent would know who Trevor had been working with. "About that," she told him. "He left the message on the machine Wednesday, and he left just after the company came to swap over the box of cash. I think he was trying to follow them."

"I should never have let him get involved in this," Crenel grumbled. "Should have believed him when he said it was real."

"I was the one who convinced you to let him do it," Penny pointed out. "But really, do you think he would have dropped it if you'd said no?"

"Smartass." The agent fell silent. "Look, you kids are killing us in the field, and you know Trevor better than anyone at the bureau. Will you take this on? You've got a better chance of finding him than anyone I have."

"Of course," Penny agreed quickly. "Officially, right? I

don't know what equipment we'll need, but when we do, I don't want to be held up with requisitions."

"I'll tell everyone involved that you have access to the lot, requests be damned." Penny waited while he had another muffled conversation, probably with the dean. "You find him, Penny. Find him fast."

CHAPTER TWELVE

Penny spent the next hours frantically researching. When Crenel arrived back at the Academy, Penny briefed him on what she had learned, both about Trevor's last movements and the case itself.

"Polybius was an urban legend from the eighties," she began. "Basically, a game released by a non-existent company with dubious origins. Few people claimed to have seen or played it. All the accounts are second hand, but not long after people started talking about the game itself, a second rumor started."

She slid a sheet of paper toward Agent Crenel and Dean March. "This is the timeline. Within weeks of the original rumors cropping up, gamers were claiming that Polybius was, in fact, released as a kind of mind control or social experiment by the US government. The purpose was unclear, but most stories agree it was a very cloak and dagger, area 51-styled operation designed to harvest information about those who played it."

"I've made some calls," Crenel told her. "I can assure

you, this was *never* a government project. It just doesn't exist."

"Doesn't matter." Penny nodded at Boots, who had accompanied her to the meeting. "It's real now."

Crenel hissed a breath through his teeth. "Goddamn it. Gods and ghosts? Sure. They make sense to me. But all this technological myth is just bullshit."

"I didn't hear you say that about the million-dollar chain letter, dear," Dean March cut in smoothly.

"That's different!" Crenel snapped. "Chain letters have been around for centuries. Basic superstition. This? This is insane."

"You mean you're too old to understand it, and you wish it would go away and stop bothering you," she replied, smiling.

Crenel grumbled something under his breath. "So, what do we know about the machines?"

It was Penny's turn to curse. "Fuck-all. Sorry, Dean March."

"Not a bother, dear. The circumstances warrant a relaxation of that particular rule." She eyeballed her husband. "For some of us, anyway."

Penny continued, "Tony said the machines at his café are serviced weekly. The goons come in, empty the money, and go. Every now and then, they remove the whole machine. When that happens, it appears again overnight."

"Appears?" Crenel asked skeptically.

Penny nodded. "Literally. Tony checked his security footage. The corner it sits in is empty at a minute to midnight, and bam, there it is as soon as the date clicks over."

"And he didn't think to ask where it bloody came from?" Crenel ignored the dean's tsk.

"He did get some information," Penny continued. "Business name, postal address. I have a feeling it'll turn out to be fake, though. If these really are spooks—the urban legend version of them, anyway—they wouldn't exactly go giving out the address of their headquarters, would they?"

"They might have a front in case of inquiries," Crenel mused. "If it's manned, it may lead us to the organization itself. We can only hope."

"Anyway, Red is helping me track down what little information we have." Penny glanced at her notepad. "Cisco is canvassing the businesses around town to try and find the other machines. The next machine service at the café isn't until Wednesday. I *really* hope we don't have to wait until then to find anything concrete."

"You're sure he said he was okay?" Crenel asked.

Penny shrugged. "You saw his message yourself. But just because he said he's fine, that doesn't mean he is."

Crenel opened his cigarettes and plucked one out, only to scowl at his wife as she deftly removed it from his fingers. "Not in here, dear."

"What's with the 'three weeks'?" Crenel asked, diverting his attention back to Penny.

All Penny could do was shrug. "Beats me."

Crenel frowned. "I also saw a million dollars in that message. What if it was a ransom demand?"

Dean March rolled her eyes behind him. "Penny has already explained that was a placeholder entry. It was there *before* Trevor's disappearance."

"Right." The agent seemed to take it as a personal

affront that the situation was so far out of his area of expertise, and that a bunch of twenty-somethings were already so far ahead in understanding that he couldn't seem to catch up. "Just keep me in the loop, okay? But if we do need a suitcase full of cash, be aware that'll take some time—and some maneuvering—to procure."

"Speaking of procurement, where is the machine now?" Penny had insisted on the arcade game being brought in for testing, and to keep it away from any other unlucky victims of whatever was going on.

Crenel looked at his phone. "GPS says they should arrive in fifteen. They'll do their own tests on it in the Academy lab. They probably won't let you near it until they're done. Don't wanna get a student blown up or anything."

"Will you let me know as soon as I can access it?" Penny asked pensively. She'd have liked to be the first person to examine it, if only to reassure herself that Trevor's odd message hadn't been changed.

"I'll make sure of it." Dean March pressed a hand on Penny's arm. "Don't worry, Penny. We know he's your friend. You will have full access to every facet of this investigation."

"Oh, will she now?" Crenel asked, looking down at his wife.

"Will she not?" The dean's voice held a note of daring.

Crenel snorted. "Of course she will, she's *running* the damn thing. But that's my call, not yours, woman."

The dean simply cocked an eyebrow at her husband, but it was enough to deflate his belligerent posture.

"Thanks, Dean. Agent Crenel." Penny turned to leave

but paused before she reached the door. "Did your mother…pass?"

"Pass?" Crenel frowned at her. "You mean, did she place?"

"Did she die? You said she only had minutes left." Penny winced at her mangled words and cringed even harder when Crenel burst out laughing.

Even Dean March couldn't smother a smile.

"I'm sure she wished she was dead by the end of it," he wheezed. "Penny, she was running a marathon. Not dying!"

"What?" The dots connected with lightning speed, and a wave of embarrassment crashed over Penny. "Oh, for crying out loud. I'm such an idiot!"

"No, dear. Professor Madera made an inquiry along similar lines." Dean March shook her head. "Knowing the way rumors spread at this Academy, I should have known better than to leave without a full and comprehensive explanation as to where I was going and why."

"How old is she?" Penny blurted without thinking. Crenel himself was as old as the hills, she was sure. How old must his *mother* be?

"Eighty-six," Crenel said proudly. "She only started running a decade ago. This is her third full marathon. I missed the last two because of work, and she's been dying to show off her new running prowess."

"That makes so much more sense." She eyed the agent. "I was beginning to think you were either a cold-hearted bastard or your mother was just awful."

"Well, you weren't entirely wrong on the first part," Crenel admitted. "But I wouldn't go so far as to celebrate the eventual passing of my mother, no matter how eccentric she's getting in her old age."

"His mother is a saint, purely by virtue of putting up with her son," Dean March stated primly. "Now, I'm sure you're eager to get started on your search, Penny. I have some contacts who may have some information as well. I'll be sure to let you know if I find anything."

"Thank you, Dean March." Penny left, letting the door swing shut behind her. "Looks like I have a busy few days ahead."

Penny leaned over Red's shoulder, squinting at the screen. "Are you sure it's them?"

She had spent the last hour pacing the Academy library while Red delved into the shell company's history. They found little information. Penny's frustration grew as their search turned up nothing except that the company was cloaked in a tight web of secrecy. Until, that was, Red found an address.

"I'm sure they *say* it's them. This is the address they gave the postal service when they registered the game machine business, but it could easily be fake." Red tapped a few keys. "Here's where it… Oh."

The map browser he had tabbed to showed "address invalid." Penny hissed a sigh of frustration. "Is it even a real street?"

Red tried again, this time leaving a building address off the query. The map popped up, a labeled satellite image showing the region the arcade distributor claimed to operate from. The area looked promising, it was full of oversized industrial buildings and warehouses. "There it is." Penny ran her finger along one of the lines crossing the screen. "Forty-two, forty-eight, fifty-six, sixty. It just… ends. Where's number sixty-four?"

Red pushed his chair back, almost rolling over Penny's toes. "Like I warned you, it's probably just a made-up location."

"What's this?" Penny pointed at a vacant lot at the end of the road, nestled behind two warehouses at the end of a driveway squeezed between them.

"Empty land?" Red shrugged. "Even if that lot had a number, it's not the sort of place you'd hide a clandestine operation. It backs right onto here—" He scrolled the screen to the left and poked a finger at a cluster of small buildings. "That's a cluster of yoga studios, organic cafes, and spiritual counselors. Do you really think a massive pseudo-government agency would plant themselves there?"

Penny narrowed her eyes at the new map section. She saw streets and buildings, but no business names. "How do you know what those buildings are?"

He gave a self-conscious laugh and pointed to a small, red-roofed row of structures at an intersection. "Me and Amelia do that sweaty sauna yoga thing there." He moved his finger over. "Then after, we grab a fresh-squeezed organic juice over here."

Penny looked at him in surprise. "You? Hot yoga? I can see Amelia getting into something like that, but Red?" She stopped, unsure how to put into words how utterly un-yoga-like Red was.

He laughed. "I'd do anything for Milly. Even twist meself into a pretzel twice a week in a box full of sweaty girls, and drink cucumber, quinoa, and goat's piss smoothies."

"They don't put goat's piss in it. Do they?" Penny had seen enough weird crazes since moving to Portland that she couldn't quite discount the suggestion completely.

Red shook his head. "Nah. It's that cilantro rubbish, I think, but it tastes like piss. It's good for your chakra or something."

"Right." Penny slid the mouse over, scrolling back to the road that should have shown the company involved with the gaming machines. "I might take a look anyway."

Red grabbed her arm. "Not alone."

"You said the address is made up." Penny faltered at the concern in his eyes. "But fine. I'll take Cisco."

"Nah. Yoga is tonight, so come with Milly and me." Red straightened and beamed a smile. "I look damn fine in those tight pants, I'll tell you now."

Wincing, Penny shook her head. "No. Please. *Anything* but yoga pants."

Red linked his arm through hers, dragging her away from the computer. "Now, don't go getting all flustered, like. Your man Cisco is a good one, even if he's not hung like a very-well-hung werewolf."

"I'm going to be sick." Penny allowed him to lead her away, though.

"I'm very happy with me girl, Amelia," he assured her. "But, it's okay to be a wee bit jealous."

Penny pulled free when they reached the hallway. "What time?" she asked. There were a few more things she could do while she waited, one of them being to call Josh and tell him she wouldn't make it in to work tonight.

"Around five. That'll give us time to investigate your missing address and still be in time for the armpit bending session." Red waved at her. "Make sure you dress for the occasion!"

CHAPTER THIRTEEN

With two hours to kill before she was due to meet Red, Penny decided to head to Paddy's. She could ask around and talk to Josh at the same time. She gave Cisco a quick buzz to let him know.

"I've found two other places that had the machines so far," Cisco told her. "A dive bar not far from Paddy's, and a local pool. They've been removed, though."

"Shit," Penny cursed. "That doesn't help us!"

"Yes, it does," Cisco countered. "Because that's not all they said. Both locations mentioned that they had a regular patron who played the machines go missing. And here's the weird thing. They both turned up three weeks later, dazed and with memory loss. And both times, *the machines went missing that night.*"

"Trevor's note said to come looking if he's not back in three weeks. He must know about those disappearances." Penny chewed her lips. "One thing. How do a random bar owner and a swimming pool attendee know so much about their customers?"

"It's a bit hard not to when the cops have grilled you about it twice," Cisco answered. She could hear the excitement in his voice. "The M.O. was the same in both cases. Both times, the victim went out to the venue—the one at the pool was last seen by a lifeguard, the other had sent a text message to his girlfriend saying he'd meet her at the bar. She was late, though, and an attendant remembered seeing her man at the arcade, no one remembered him leaving. Then, nothing for a couple of days. Family and friends called in the police, who showed photos around, jogging a few memories."

"Where did they turn up?" Penny asked, half expecting them to have been dropped by the side of the road, hogtied and beat up.

"Where they vanished from." Cisco sounded triumphant. "Early morning, prior to opening. No one saw how they got there."

"Are they okay?" Penny asked, alarmed. "Were they hurt?"

"Amnesia. At first, neither remembered who they were. It came back to them over the course of an hour or so, as they recognized faces and surroundings." Cisco paused. "The pool had their guy's face on a flyer, so they figured him out pretty fast. The other one almost got carted off as a crazy homeless trespasser, but his girlfriend happened to be driving past on her way to work, and was keeping an eye out."

"Why didn't we know about this?" Penny groaned. "We could have warned Trevor off his crazy plan!"

Cisco sighed. "It's just...not that weird. A drunk

wandering off and coming back looking like he'd been on a two-day bender?"

"At a pool?" Penny asked dryly.

"*That* guy was only eighteen. His parents thought maybe he'd run off like he had once before." Cisco paused. "Do you think the cops will let us talk to them?"

"I'll get Crenel on it." Penny quickly rattled off her own plan to hit the bar. "If this thing is out of the Veil, surely someone at Paddy's knows about it."

"Let's hope that hunch pays off."

Cisco ended the call and Penny grabbed her purse. She headed out the door only to catch Agent Crenel on his way down before her.

"I need to speak to you," she called after him.

He spun and waited for her. "That's good because I need to speak to you too. Did you email me that account information?"

Penny nodded. The scant details Tony had been able to share included the bank details where he was to deposit a small amount to cover damage to the machines while in his care. "A couple of hours ago. You didn't get it?"

Crenel grimaced, digging out his phone. "I've been too busy to check. But, one of my buddies on the Nigerian Myth task force agreed to take a look for us."

"That's the new department opened to deal with all the princes and lawyers popping up?" Penny asked.

"The one and only." Crenel stared at the glowing screen in his hand, his thumb scrolling for a moment before he grunted. "Yeah, I've got it."

He went to leave, but Penny grabbed his arm. "My turn," she reminded him. She rattled off the information

Cisco had given her. "I know it's a long shot if their memories have been wiped, but can we track them down and ask them some questions?"

"I'll make it happen." Without saying goodbye, he stabbed at his phone again and put it to his ear. "Karen? I need you to track down a couple of kidnap vics for me. Yeah, we need them back in for questioning." His voice trailed off as he strode away.

Buoyed by the feeling that progress was being made, Penny went on her way to Paddy's bar. Once there, she accepted a shot of whiskey from the leprechaun gratefully.

"Wee lass, ye look like ye've had a day." Paddy raised his own glass and clinked it against Penny's.

"I have." Penny sighed, dreading the thought of going through her story a dozen times over again as Mythers filtered in and out of the bar. "Look, I'm not here for a social visit. I need information."

"Paddy has a finger on the pulse of Portland, to be sure. What it is yer wantin' to know?" He waved absently at a trio of fairies that flitted past.

"Back before you crossed over, did you ever hear about any secret government organizations?"

Paddy rubbed his chin as he thought. "Well. If they be secret organizations, wouldn't Paddy knowin' about them make them not so secret?"

Penny groaned. "This isn't the time for jokes, Paddy. What about a computer game or an arcade machine?"

Paddy took another moment, sipping his drink, brow creased in a wrinkled frown. "Nope," he told her at last. "Can't say that I have."

"Can you ask around?" Penny asked. "The game is

called Polybius, it's been popping up in cafes and bars and other places around Portland. Some kind of shady organization is behind it—and they've taken a friend of mine."

Paddy brightened. "Was it just in Portland?"

Penny nodded. "We can't find reports anywhere else, but that makes sense as it was an old local legend from thirty or forty years ago. Does that change anything?"

Paddy nodded eagerly. "I'm what ye call a world-wisely leprechaun. Ye see, I wasn't actually from Portland to begin with. I wouldn't have heard about such things unless one of me crew has mentioned it since bein' here."

"You're not from Portland?" Penny asked. She had assumed the small, green man had been conceived on his side of the veil from the ancient bar's logo.

"No, lass. Wee Paddy came from an old family farm near Hobsonville. Brought the stories over from the home country, they did."

Penny sat back, examining him. "Why did you leave?"

"I'm Irish." Paddy elaborated when he saw Penny's look of bewilderment. "We love ourselves a bit of adventure, lass. Not much to be found on a wheat farm that was bought out by some prick of an Englishman a whole generation ago."

Penny let the matter drop, resolving to ask him more at a later date. "Who can I ask about the local legends then?"

"Have you spoke to Tilly?" Paddy drained his glass and slid it across the table.

Penny frowned. "Who's Tilly?"

"Oh, right. The poor lass doesn't have a corporeal body. Well, you might need some assistance to be talking to her, but she will be the lass to see. She knows everything about this old city." Paddy stood up and made to leave.

"You can't just leave me with that!" Penny grabbed him by the collar and hauled him back to the table. "Who is Tilly? And how do I find her?"

"You found her already, lass, you just didn't know it at the time." Paddy gave her a mischievous wink. "She's a kitchen hand at the Baghdad. I believe the two of you met briefly around this time last year?"

Penny stared at him, stunned. Then, she picked up her glass and drink her whiskey in a single gulp. "Thanks!"

It wasn't long until her rendezvous with Red and Amelia. Tilly would have to wait. Still, Penny tapped off a quick message to Agent Crenel.

I need to get into the Bagdad kitchen. While they're closed, preferably. Can you help with that?

Crenel messaged back almost instantly.

Is this even related to your case?

Penny rolled her eyes as she typed her reply.

I wouldn't ask if it wasn't.

Crenel's reply was short.

Fine. I'll see if DeLouise still has the owner's number.

From what Paddy had said, Tilly was one of the friendly, protective ghosts who had helped to fight off a malicious entity the previous year. Unlike the grotesque specter that had been summoned in the downstairs bathroom, the kitchen ghosts adhered closer to the presentation of a poltergeist. They couldn't be seen or heard. They could manipulate objects, though.

"I wonder if she could use a pen and paper?" Penny mused. Pushing the thought aside, she glanced around the bar. It was too early for the evening rush to have started, but Esmeralda sat at the bar, swinging her stumpy legs and buttoned boots under her barstool.

Penny approached her carefully. When she had first started working at Paddy's, she had had to evict Esmeralda a grand total of four times for inciting unrest and for just plain being a bitch. Recently, however, they had come to an understanding. Esmeralda kept her gripes about the less-accepted Mythers that frequented the bar to herself, and Penny made sure the fairy godmother made it safely to a cab each night without face planting in the gutter in a drunken stupor.

"Esmeralda?" Penny slid onto the barstool next to the cantankerous fairy.

"Yes?" The old woman's voice was cold, and the thin eyebrow that arched at Penny made her feel like she was getting in trouble at school.

Thankfully, months of dealing with the old hag had taught Penny exactly how to deal with her. "I need your help. Before you refuse, you should know what's at stake." Penny paused dramatically. "A young man, right this very moment, is wishing for a miracle."

Esmerelda blinked. "A miracle?"

Penny nodded gravely. "A miracle. He's praying...I mean, dreaming for a powerful being, one who can protect him". Careful girl, you don't want her to brush this off as Gabriel's problem.

"And what is this young man's name?" As hard as she might try to feign disinterest, Esmerelda was practically twitching in her seat.

"Trevor," Penny told her. "Trevor White."

Esmerelda's lips pressed into a light line as she warred between her deep loathing of the pretentious girl who insisted on putting the Fairy Godmother in her place over and over again and fulfilling the very duty she was created for. "He's not one of mine," Esmerelda told her at last. "I can't interfere directly."

Penny smiled sweetly. "Of course. All I need is some information." She quickly asked about *Polybius* and the shady group behind it.

Esmerelda pursed her lips. "I don't know of it, but I shall ask around." Her eyes narrowed and her chin lifted. Looking down her nose at Penny, she added, "For the boy, of course."

"Thank you." Not willing to push her luck, Penny left the woman sipping her scotch and glaring at the other patrons through wire-rimmed spectacles.

CHAPTER FOURTEEN

The abandoned house at the end of Robinson Road loomed over the empty concrete lot like an aging matriarch. Penny scrutinized it, noting the soft flutter of a torn curtain through one smashed window, and the gentle tap of a shutter in the afternoon breeze.

"Why would they advertise they're here?" Amelia asked, gesturing at a sign on the wire fence that read *Stay Out, Mythological Activity On-Site*

Penny considered it. It certainly didn't fit with the MO of a secret facility. "Maybe it's reverse psychology?" The explanation felt as weak as it sounded, but she had come this far. Her gut wouldn't let her rest until she'd checked out this lead.

"This looks like a really bad idea," Red put in. "Look at that place! It's full of busted boards and rusty nails." He tugged at the forest green tights covering his legs. "I'm going to snag me nice pants!"

Amelia groaned. "When I asked him to come to yoga

with me, I thought he'd say no. I never expected it to make him this...*precious*."

"I'm just doing what I need to support me lass, lass." Red grinned. "If you want me to follow Penny into the bowels of the creepy, haunted house, I will. Just remember, if an evil splinter rips a hole in me duds and you see my crack, it's not *my* fault."

"Why did I ever agree to bring him?" Penny asked Amelia.

Amelia shrugged. "Beats me, I would have left him at home. In fact, I'd take a dead goldfish over him." Red grunted but she ignored it. "Anyway, you're stuck with him now, so are we going in?"

The house sat at the approximate location of sixty-six Robinson road. It was still quite a bit short of the listed address they wanted, but it was as close as they were going to get.

"Let's do it." Penny tugged the strap of her backpack, adjusting the weight. She'd already taken out a flashlight and her handgun, and clipped some specialty magazines to her belt—silver bullets, exploding holy water cartridges, and one containing a single drop of *eitr*, a substance from Norse mythology strong enough to kill a god. Unfortunately, it probably wouldn't work on much else.

It felt strange to be missing her other bag, but Boots had given her a brisk hiss and shoved Penny toward the dorm room door before diving into a pile of blankets. *It's not like we're joined at the hip*, Penny reassured herself. *She probably just wants to nap.*

Penny squeezed through the loosely chained gates, holding the gap open when she was through so Amelia and

Red could follow. She waited patiently as Amelia helped Red untangle a thread of polyester that caught on a loose wire, threatening to unravel the flimsy fabric covering his backside.

"Sorry," Red grumbled.

"It's fine," Penny assured him, grabbing his arm. "I really am glad you're here."

"Yeah," Amelia affirmed, kissing his cheek. "If nothing else, the sight of your holey yoga pants will scare off any vampires."

Snorting, Red forged ahead, traipsing up the long gravel drive toward the house.

Amelia pulled back as they reached the rotting porch, tugging Penny and Red behind the empty husk of a dead tree trunk. "We need to go over some rules," she told them.

"Rules?" Red asked. "Shoot the bad guys, not ourselves. Find Trevor, and run."

"We don't know if this is even the right place," Amelia insisted. "Look, this dump has all the trappings of a haunted house. Or a possessed one. Or...remember that mansion that popped up in New York with the dolls on a murder rampage?"

Penny shook her head. "How the hell did I miss that one?"

Brushing it off, Amelia continued. "What I'm saying is, we could be walking into anything. We have to promise to stick together in there, no matter what. No going after creepy noises in the basement or following sweet little girls down random hallways. Got it?"

"Got it." Red saluted her. "But when did you become an expert on this sort of thing?"

Amelia flicked her hair and gave him a cheeky smirk. "I started a blog as part of my course. It's an offshoot from my local witch-hunting site. 'The Haunting: Where to find the best haunted houses and how to survive them.' It's getting quite popular."

"Really?" Penny knew Amelia had always been into the online blogging thing. She had started fashion blogs, study blogs, and one, apparently, chronicling the journey of sharing a dorm room with an Aussie girl and a snake. She hadn't mentioned this new venture, though.

"Really. Now, any questions?" Amelia waited, then nodded after a moment of silence. "Let's go."

The front door had swollen with age. Red leaned against it but shook his head. "I can give it a shove, but it'll be noisy. Milly?"

Amelia had already thrown a leg through a nearby window that was missing its glass. "Quiet as mice, guys."

Penny slipped through next, and the two girls each grabbed one of Red's arms as he awkwardly stuffed his tall frame through the small opening. One of his feet caught the windowsill on the way through, but Penny hauled him up before he thudded on the floorboards.

Panting, Red found his balance and gave her a thumbs-up before slipping a flashlight from his belt. He shone the narrow beam around the room.

The long sitting room might have been beautiful once. Heavy wooden chairs sat by boarded-up windows, coated in thick layers of dust. A side table held a tarnished silver tea set, and a half-complete tapestry lay on the floor, loose threads still attached to a rusted needle.

"This place must be *full* of bugs," Amelia whispered. She

pointed at a moth-eaten cushion. "Gods, I hope we don't find any spiders in here."

Penny chuckled lightly. "Mate, the spiders here have nothing on the ones back home. If we find any, just leave them to me."

"Aye, but what if it's an eight-foot-tall arachnid with a million babies, that eats human heads for breakfast?" Red asked. Amelia slapped him in the chest and he gasped. "Well, it might happen!"

"Asshole." Amelia nodded to the door on the other side of the room. "Just don't touch anything, okay?"

Murmuring agreement, Penny placed a hand on the old brass knob. It turned easily and the door swung open, as smooth as if it had been oiled yesterday.

"Which way?" Penny asked. The narrow corridor ahead led to a staircase. Two closed doors lined the left side, and a niche behind the stairs glowed with a soft light.

"If it's a haunted house, the bogeyman will be in the attic or basement, most likely." Amelia gestured to the nearest door. "But we're hoping it's something else, right? We need to be thorough."

The door, however, was locked. Penny eyed it, then pulled her gun out and attached the silencer. "Stand back."

"Don't shoot it!" Red snapped. "You know that doesn't work in real life!"

Kneeling, Penny gave him a withering glare. "I'm picking the lock, you numpty. The gun is for whatever is on the other side." She set it on the floor, safety engaged, and drew a lock-picking set from her belt. A minute later, she put the set away, picked up her gun, and pointed it at the door. "Careful," she whispered.

The brass knob turned smoothly. This door wasn't as quiet as the previous one. It squeaked open loudly, thudding to a stop only halfway. "It looks like it's been tossed," Red remarked. His light was trained on the floor, where piles of moldering books were strewn in a pile.

"Uh-huh." Penny edged around the door to see why it wouldn't open properly. She kicked away a fallen chair and pushed the door back, latching it open. "Or a fight broke out."

Dust plumed as Amelia pulled the long, heavy curtains back to reveal ancient, crackling oil paintings lined with cobwebs. "Ugh. I told you there would be spiders."

Penny scanned the room. "That chair is broken." She pointed to the one that had blocked the door. "Where is its missing leg? And whatever tipped over that desk must be strong."

The ornate desk had landed crookedly, one corner propped up by an old book wedged underneath. Red walked over and gripped the bottom edge with his fingers. He grunted, then let go. "It's a heavy bastard, all right. Can I ask you ladies for some assistance?"

Penny reluctantly tucked her weapon back into her belt. Between them, they managed to tip the desk back up, though one drawer clattered to the floor in the process. "So much for being quiet," Penny grumbled. "Why are we tidying up this mess, exactly?"

Red pointed at the drawer that had dislodged. "Clues." He picked up some papers that had fallen out and held them up to the light from the windows. "Huh. Just some old letters. Too old to be our goons."

He grabbed the now-empty drawer and slid it into the

desk. Then, frowning, he slid it back out. He knocked on the bottom.

"Hidden compartment?" Amelia asked.

"Aye." Red set it on top of the desk and pulled out a knife. He slid it carefully into the drawer base.

A page fluttered in the breeze.

Hold up. Penny turned to look for the source. *There is no breeze.*

A book flew across the room, aimed at Red's back. It thudded between his shoulder blades, knocking him toward the desk. "Ow! Who bloody threw that?"

"Ghosts!" Penny yelled as she dropped into a defensive stance. "Get that thing open so we can get out of here!" A second book launched into the air, and she knocked it off its path with a well-placed kick. The book fell to the ground, inanimate.

A third book rustled. Penny hit this one with the flat of her hand, taking another one out with her foot seconds later. Grabbing the chair, Penny yelled to Amelia. "Get behind the desk!"

The projectile books were all coming from one corner of the room. Backhanding one, Penny lunged with the broken chair. The momentary distraction let a small hardback past, and Red yelped as it slammed into the back of his head. "Pointy little prick!"

Swinging the chair, Penny took out two more, eyeing a third that hung suspended in midair. "Go on," she hissed at it. "Try me."

It did. The book plunged forward, swooping left to avoid the chair back Penny lifted as a shield. It wasn't quick enough to avoid the kick that followed, though.

"Take that, poltergeist prick." Penny regretted her words when twenty books slowly lifted into the air. "Um, Red? You're not done, are you? Because—"

"Got it!" Red hollered.

"Duck!" Penny yelled. The books flew at them, and Penny tossed the chair blindly into their path as she dove to the side. Amelia squealed and Red grunted as they clattered to the ground.

"Run!" Red yelled.

A large atlas slammed into the door, flinging it shut. The door bounced back, a tiny, leather-bound novel caught in the jam. Penny slipped through first and wedged her body between the door and its frame to hold their exit open.

Red dove under Penny's arms as Amelia wielded a lump of wood like a baseball bat. She slammed one book, then another, edging back toward the door.

"You show 'em, princess!" Red yelled.

Amelia roared as she hit another missile, ricocheting it to take out three others that had lifted off the floor. She dove for Penny, who yanked her out of the room moments before the door slammed closed. A rumbling clatter sounded on the other side as books pelted into it.

Then, silence.

"That was a blast," Amelia commented, panting. "I used to hate softball as a kid, but then I never thought it'd come in handy like that."

"You saved my ass!" Red kissed her. "Thanks, love."

Amelia hugged him. "Did you get what you were after?"

Red held up the proceeds of his search. He passed three sheets of paper to Penny and dangled a long gold chain with a black stone pendant in front of Amelia. "Is that suitably creepy, love?"

Amelia reached out, then pulled back. "Yeah. We probably don't want to touch that."

Red slipped the prize into a plastic bag and tucked it away. "What does the letter say?"

Penny pressed the paper against the wall while Red pointed his flashlight at it. Penny skimmed the first page.

Dear Mister Perkins,

I trust this letter finds you well. Now, enough of this nonsense. Release my son from your custody and be done with it. You damn well know he didn't kill Jonas Weatherbee, and God help you if you see an innocent man hang for another's crimes.

Yours, Anna Marple.

A signature scrawled at the bottom ended the letter. When Red and Amelia nodded, she slid it away to read the next one.

Mister Perkins,

You did not respond to my letter. Please, my Richard is innocent. You cannot let him hang for this crime that he did not commit.

Now I know I am not the most well-regarded woman in town. I know you've heard those rumors, but that's all they are. I attend church on a Sunday and have a respectable income of twelve dollars a week cleaning for Mister Jones. I'm no witch, Mister Perkins, and you'd best not let my son take the burden of those accusations against me.

Please, Mister Perkins, do the right thing. The pastor says that God keeps his children safe, and I pray it is true. I find it hard to keep that faith when my boy, my Richard, is sentenced to death.

This necklace is the only thing of value I have. Take it. Use it as your security if you wish, but save my boy.

Sincerely,

Anna Marple.

"Ouch." Penny could almost feel the animosity bleeding from the jagged letters beneath her fingers. "That poor woman, she sounds so desperate. I wonder if he really was innocent?"

The third letter was short. A couple of hastily scrawled lines, smudged in places and marred by creases in the paper as if it had been crumpled, then smoothed.

Rot in hell, Perkins. You killed my son and took everything from me. By the unholy powers I possess, I will see your town burned to the ground.

"This house is definitely haunted," Red remarked. "I can feel it in me jellies."

"Not necessarily," Amelia murmured.

Red scoffed. "What, you think it's just a boring old house full of flying books?"

Amelia pointed at the letters. "If Anna really *was* a witch, maybe she's the entity that crossed the Veil."

"Oh, wonderful." Penny glanced back at the silent room. "Ghosts *and* a vengeful witch."

"But no clandestine organizations that kidnap twenty-year-old geeks who like video games," Red pointed out.

"Unless it's all a front," Penny shot back.

"You know," Amelia suggested. "It might be a trap. What if the spooks know about the house and gave this address to lure in idiots like us? Maybe they know something malevolent is here, and they think it'll take out anyone who comes looking for them."

The thought made Penny's gut churn. "Amelia, a few flying books wouldn't do much to stop anyone. Do you think…"

"Something worse is around the corner?" Red suggested. "Let's make like a genius and get the hell out of this weird house before we die."

Nodding, Penny headed back across the hallway to the sitting room. She opened the door. Then, she stepped back.

Amelia stepped on her heels. "Why'd you stop?"

"I must have opened the wrong door." Penny stepped back, confused. This was the only door on this side of the hallway.

"What?" Red laughed. "Don't be daft, Penny. This is the…" he paused as he realized the layout had changed. "*Oh.* Where did the windows go?"

The sitting room was exactly as they had left it, right down to the discarded tapestry and ancient tea set. The room, however, was windowless.

"That's not even possible," Penny insisted. "Is it?"

"Guess we're stuck here until the end," Amelia moaned.

"The end?" Penny gripped the doorframe. "You mean until we die?"

"No. Well, no." Amelia plastered a false smile on. "Just until we meet the evil entity trapping us here and defeat it."

"Or die trying." Red walked over to the wall across from them and punched the blank spot that should have held a window. A chunk of plaster fell away to reveal red bricks. "That's what you *really* mean to say, isn't it?"

Amelia's smile faltered. "Look, statistically, people are really unlikely to die in a haunted house," she insisted.

She's lying through her teeth. "How do those statistics

hold up once you're already *in* a haunted house?" Penny asked.

Smile gone, Amelia glared at her. "Fine. We're basically screwed. We have about a twelve percent chance of surviving."

"Oh." Penny checked her belt, reloaded her gun—since the holy water had a decent chance of being helpful here—and opened the sitting-room door. "Twelve percent isn't that bad. I thought it'd be a lot worse, actually."

"Seriously?" Red stared at her, mouth hanging open.

Penny gestured with her gun. "How many people *statistically* enter a haunted house after three semesters at a school that trains you to deal with shit like this? And how many of those are armed to the teeth with holy water, salt, and flamethrowers?"

"Not many, I bet." Amelia grinned and drew a small cross from her own pack. "Not to mention, we're really smart, and we know stuff. Like, if there's an actual Salem-era witch involved in this mess, we should go the religious combat route. We good?"

Red grumbled but agreed. "But I'm gonna point out there's something else in common here." He held up a hand, raising a finger with each point. "Anna Marple is a woman." Two more fingers. "And Penny and Amelia? Both girls. You two dragged me into this." He threw his hands up. "Women are trouble!"

CHAPTER FIFTEEN

Back in the hallway, Penny cracked open the door to the next room. Dust covered the floor, and an old high-backed chair sat in the corner. The emptiness sent a shiver across her skin. "Nothing here." She backed out and closed the door behind her. "Where to next? The eerie glow of the afterlife, or the stairway to death?"

"Not funny," Red grumbled. "I just want to take the fastest path out of this place."

"Impossible." Amelia headed toward the niche behind the stairs. "This kind of event is usually linked to a set sequence. Like the letters. We had to discover those first, it's a clue to what's inside. Even if you skip something important, it'll come back round to get you."

"You know that's not at all reassuring, right?" Red loaded his holy water cartridge into his gun and holstered it. He replaced it with a small flamethrower, bouncing it in his palm.

"Don't use that here!" Penny snatched it out of his hand. "This whole place will go up in flames, with *us* in it!"

Crestfallen, Red accepted the flamethrower back from Penny and put it away. "Fine. But I'm burning this hellhole to the ground when we leave. I've got bruises all over me back, and we're not done yet."

Amelia cocked her head. "I wonder if you can even burn a fire witch? It's either poetic justice and will work like a charm, or she'll be completely immune.

"And just like that, this place gets even creepier." Penny headed toward the staircase. Instead of going up, she peeked around the back. "Looks like this leads to a kitchen."

The kitchen was dark, the shadows deepened by a thin coating of sooty grime on the walls and windows instead of the pale dust coating the other rooms.

Red ran a finger over the tiled counter, leaving a clean streak of white and blue porcelain exposed. "Someone needs to get rid of the maid," he remarked, screwing up his face. He wiped the dirty fingertip on his pants, leaving a black mark. "Aw, now I'm all dirty!"

"That's smoke damage," Penny told him. "Maybe the oven flue got blocked." She leaned over the ancient wood-fired stove and stuck her head in, then drew it out, coughing. "Ugh. Blocked by a family of spiders. I think I just snorted a cobweb."

"What's that in the corner of the room?" Amelia pointed at a cluster of blackened debris that came to her knee. The ceiling above had crumbled away, revealing rotted floorboards above.

Penny stepped back, running her eyes over the room. "The soot and scorch marks are all coming from that direction." She waved a hand at the ceiling above. "And the damage is worse above it. Maybe that was the origin of the fire?"

Red nudged the heap with a toe and his breath caught in his throat. "I don't think it was the fuel." He crept closer, then pulled back. "I think it was the victim."

Penny's gut twisted as she realized the shape of the burned heap was curled into a fetal position. "It's…a *body?*"

The black shape twitched, and Amelia squealed. "It's *alive!*"

"It's not—" Penny's protest stuck in her throat as she realized Amelia was right. Penny yanked her gun from her belt, pointing it at the blackened, twisted shape that rose from the scorched remnants.

Two eyes shone malevolently from a skeletal face. A gaping maw formed by broken teeth and melted lips opened, and a hoarse scream filled the room.

Red screamed back, a shrill, ear-piercing sound that drowned out the damaged vocals of the ghoul before them. He grabbed a heavy cast iron pan from the cooktop and hurled it at the specter. The pan slammed through leathered flesh and brittle bone to clatter on the wall behind it. The ghoul crumpled to the ground.

Red stood over it, breathing heavily.

"Wow, babe. You, uh, really showed that thing." Amelia's lips twitched but she held onto her composure. "Was the high-pitched scream a distraction technique?"

Red gave her a wavering grin. "Sorry. I kind of panicked."

"Intentional or not, it worked," Penny told him. She

patted Red on the back. "It's okay. We won't tell anyone you shrieked like a girl."

"Hey, I didn't see any girls screaming." Amelia winked at her boyfriend. "But I won't tell, either."

Red wiped a sooty hand over his sweaty forehead, leaving a smudge. "Right. Focus, Red. You've got this." His shoulders wriggled as a shiver wracked him, but he shook it off. "It's just a house. It's a creepy as fuck, haunted to the bones, probably witch-infested…house."

"Can we get a move on?" Penny lowered her gun and clicked the safety back on. "The sooner we're done here, the sooner I can curl into a ball and cry tears of relief."

Amelia nodded. "This place really does have an atmosphere, doesn't it?"

A quick search of the kitchen revealed little of interest, the contents being mostly kitchen equipment and a few intact jars that once held preserved food but were now filled with an opaque, gelatinous substance.

Once Amelia was satisfied they would learn nothing new, the trio moved on. "I haven't seen a basement," she said slowly. "So whatever the end goal is, it's probably up there somewhere."

Penny drew her weapon again, taking point as they went up the narrow steps. The boards were spongy beneath her feet, and one cracked loudly under her weight. "Be careful," she whispered to Red. "You don't want to fall through."

A tiny landing at the top led to a single door, striking in its sparkling perfection. Somehow, despite the rot through the rest of the building, this door was untouched by age, unmarred by the stains of the ancient fire.

"This is it." Amelia gestured to the door. "This is the payload. Whatever is in there will either kill us or let us out."

Penny twisted the brass knob. The door swung open cleanly to reveal an old fashioned office. A desk, not unlike the damaged one downstairs, sat across from her. A plump, balding man sat at the desk, flicking idly through a stack of papers on his desk. He dipped a long pen into a glass ink jar, then scrawled on the page before him.

"Anna, I simply see no way to intervene." Despite the man's age, his eyes were bright and intelligent, if scornful and hard. "There were witnesses. I'm afraid your Richard was guilty. Now, he faces the judgment of a higher court." He looked back down at his desk, flicking the paper aside casually. "May God have mercy on his soul."

"Don't you lie to me, Perkins."

Penny jerked back, spinning around to look for the source of the voice. A dark-haired woman stepped out of a shadowed corner, her face drawn and eyes rimmed with red. Anna Marple.

"Jonas Timms had eyes for Catherine. You know he did." Anna spat on the floor. "He wanted Richard gone so he could have her for himself."

Perkins made no reply, simply slipping another sheet of paper to one side.

"Damn you!" Anna shot over to his desk and thrust her arm forward, her fingers splayed. "You can't ignore me, you bastard!"

Perkins gave a strangled scream as his body was lifted into the air and slammed against the ceiling, his limbs pinned by an unseen force.

"Do you know how it feels to lose your light, your reason to live?" Anna shrieked. "Know now. Laura is dead, burned to ashes like my son."

Perkins heaved a tight gasp, his terror crumbling to grief. "No." His whispered plea fell on deaf ears. "No! She is with child!"

"If she was, then they are both dead." Anna hissed the words, unmoved by the tears streaming down the man's face. "And now it is your turn. Perhaps you will see them at the gates of Hell."

Anna flicked her hand and Perkins erupted into flames, writhing and screaming as his body contorted in agony. Flames licked at the ceiling, racing toward the books that lined the nearby walls.

"I will burn you to the ground! You and everyone else in this hell-forsaken town." Anna's eyes reflected the glow of the fire as they turned to Penny. "All of you."

Flames shot from her fingers but Red was faster, swooping in front of Penny with a shield of silver foil. "Good thing she's never heard of an emergency blanket, eh?" He grinned as the roaring fire rained against the protective sheet.

The heat lessened, and Anna let out a yell of frustration.

Penny cocked her weapon. "Where's Amelia?" She had to yell over the crackling and hiss of burning wood.

"Behind the desk," Red told her.

Penny nodded to show she'd heard. "You're on defense!"

Red nodded and dropped even closer to the ground, taking the sheet with him. Penny blinked her burning eyes, exposed to a fresh wave of scorching heat. *There.* A shadow moved in the smoke, and she let off two rounds. The quick *pop-pop* of the gun was punctuated by the sound of the specialist bullets exploding into wood, followed by a hiss of evaporating water. Then, just as Penny had given up hope, there was a wail of pain.

Penny shrank down behind the fire blanket, and Red pulled it over her head.

"Did you get her, lass?"

Penny shook her head. "I think I hit her with some holy steam, but it sure didn't sound like the throes of death." She couldn't be sure how much damage had been done, but now they knew at least one of their weapons worked. "Let's move out."

Penny crouched beneath the billowing smoke and pointed her flashlight toward the mayor's desk. She clicked it on and off a few times, signaling to Amelia that they were retreating. A sequence of flashes came back, showing she had understood.

Huddled under the fireproof blankets, they fled. Penny paused only to yank the door closed behind her. "Ouch!" She sucked her fingers, which were singed from the hot doorknob.

"Downstairs," Red suggested. "We can make our stand in the kitchen."

"There's no chance those water pumps work, Red." Amelia ran as she spoke, taking the stairs two at a time.

"No," he agreed. "But it's not quite as flammable as these old wooden walls. It'll hold a boat-load of blessed steam, *and* it's full of sharp things."

Penny grinned. "You're thinking we need to go Queen of Hearts?"

"Off with her head!" Red jumped, sailing over the last

four steps and spinning on one foot with a grin. "Then the old bitch can burn herself down!"

Penny slapped her palm on his as she passed him in a high five. "Let's hope the whole building goes down with her."

"Don't steal all my fun." Red followed Penny and Amelia into the kitchen. He quickly glanced around, then armed himself with a cast iron cooking pot.

Penny scanned the room, even as she felt the seconds ticking by. An evil cackle filled the air, but she ignored it.

Something sharp. She spied a small paring knife. *Too small. I need something with a bit of weight behind it. Something that will slice through—* A grin spread across Penny's face when she spotted what she needed. *Perfect.*

A heavy weight slammed into the kitchen door. Penny gripped the cleaver in her hand and edged behind the heavy table in the center of the room. Another slam, this one hard enough to dislodge a pin in one of the heavy black hinges.

Silence.

The door exploded, metal bracing and ancient wood splintering as it flew across the room.

Penny threw herself under the table, flinching as something ricocheted off it. She heard Red's cry from the doorway and scrambled forward, coming to her feet to see her friend wrestling with the gruesome specter.

Anna Marple's face had aged and withered, her hair thinning to just a few grey strands sprouting from an age-spotted scalp. She bared her teeth—what was left of them —and drew back a hand, her movements strong and steady despite knobbled joints and wasting flesh.

A ball of flame flared in her palm as her other hand gripped Red's throat.

He struggled to free himself from her chokehold, his toes dangling a few inches off the floor as the witch floated in the middle of the room.

Penny wanted to react. She itched to move but forced herself to wait. She didn't have to wait long.

With a yell of victory, Amelia yanked the crone's flaming hand behind her back, caught it in a garrote, and twisted it painfully up to her shoulder blades. While Penny gripped the cleaver, waiting for the perfect moment to strike, Red dropped to the floor and grabbed the pot he had dropped in the attack.

He swung it, smashing cast iron into the witch's skull. Anna screamed in anguish, her cries bubbling as blood poured from her mouth. Her eye swung from a sticky tendon, dangling by her cheek beneath the cavernous indent in her head.

Red adjusted his grip and swung the pot again, this time bringing it down on the witch's head like an oversized hat. He pinned her down, and Amelia grabbed her legs. Despite the old woman's injuries, she writhed and flailed.

Penny let out a grunt of frustration. "Hold her still!" If she didn't execute the move perfectly, well. It wouldn't be the witch who was executed.

"She's stronger than she looks," Red snapped. He had all his weight on the pot, but it still shuddered and scraped on the stone floor as Anna struggled to free herself.

If you want something done right... Penny threw herself across the old woman's body, using her knees to pin the witch's chest. She ignored the claws that pierced her shirt and scratched her belly.

Penny raised the cleaver. Then, she brought it down with all her might.

CHAPTER SIXTEEN

Penny stared at the smoldering building, her jaw clenched. She pulled away from Amelia's touch on her arm.

"It was worth a try, lass." For once, Red spoke sincerely.

"No." Penny turned back toward her friends. "It was a waste of time. Time I could have better spent elsewhere."

"Like where?" Amelia waved a hand around. "You had no idea what you'd find here! You have other leads, but none of them are ready to be actioned. At least now you know the address was a fake or a diversion, but the outcome is the same. Now you can focus your efforts somewhere else."

"I suppose so." Penny kicked at a lump of broken concrete on the ground, then pulled out her phone. "I guess the yoga class is canceled?"

"I'm still up for it." Red looked down at the pale skin peeking through his singed and shredded tights. "I don't think my pants are, though."

"That was enough of a workout for me," Amelia told

them. "I might hit the library though—after I clean up. I was going to do it tomorrow anyway."

"Assignment?" Penny asked.

Amelia shook her head. "I'm going to put my meager skills to the test. My plan is to trawl through all the independent newspapers and local blogs to see if there's any mention of this Polybius game."

"And I'm going to rub her feet while she does it." Red shrugged. "Unless there's a better way for me to help? The next full moon is weeks away. Otherwise, I could just sniff the bastard out."

"Let's hope we find him before it comes to that." Penny straightened her shoulders. "This hunch may not have panned out, but I still have a few more cards up my sleeve."

"And a few more scars, if you don't get those healed." Amelia gestured to Penny's ruined shirt. "Make sure you get that treated, Penny. Who knows what disgusting germs those grotty fingernails were harboring."

Rather than trust Penny's good sense, Amelia accompanied her to the first aid room when they arrived back at the Academy.

"Get to it." Amelia waved at the locker that housed the Asclepius Staff. "I'll do the paperwork for you."

"You're a gem." Penny entered the six-digit code to unlock the door and grabbed the staff. She pulled up her shirt, wincing as she peeled off a bit of fabric that was stuck to her skin. Luckily, the wound looked fairly clean. The staff would take care of any bacteria, but not solid debris that would become trapped in the flesh as it healed over.

A few short minutes later, Penny felt whole again, if extremely hungry.

"I don't meet the dress standards for the dining hall like this. I'll have to change before I eat." Penny scribbled her signature on the sign out paperwork Amelia handed to her. "Are you heading down to grab dinner?"

Amelia considered a moment, then shook her head. "No. I can grab something on the way to the library with Red. I want to get started right away."

Penny nodded. In truth, she was a little relieved. "Oh, by the way, I'm going out tonight. DeLouise has organized a visit to the Bagdad for me, but I can't get in until they close."

"You're following up on the lead Paddy gave you?" Amelia grimaced. "Well, I guess it's better to go after they close than before they open. I hate early mornings."

"Same. They did offer me a morning visit, but one AM somehow sounded less awful than five." Penny gave Amelia an impulsive hug as they headed upstairs together. "Thanks for coming to check out that horrible house with me."

They reached their room, and Penny turned the doorknob. She pushed, but it didn't open.

"Huh?" She jiggled the handle and shoved harder. This time, the door cracked open a tiny sliver. "Something is blocking the door."

"How?" Amelia added her weight to it. "Is someone in there?"

The answer came as a hiss. "Boots?" Penny slapped a hand on the door. "You open this door right now, Miss. So help me I'll—"

There was a scrape and a clatter, and the door fell open.

Penny stepped inside and righted the fallen chair. "Did you barricade the door?" she asked, incredulous. "Why? *How?* You're a snake!"

Boots' hiss turned from apologetic to offended.

"Fine. You're a highly intelligent serpent. But what the hell?" Penny perched on the edge of her bed and gestured for Boots to join her. "Was someone trying to get in?"

Boots nodded.

"And you thought they wanted to hurt you?" she asked.

Boots waggled her head in a dipping, swaying movement that was somewhere between a yes and a no.

"I don't even know what that means." Penny sighed. "You poor thing. You were scared, weren't you?"

Boots shook her head. Then, she looked down and nodded.

Penny cupped the serpent's head and touched their noses together. "Whatever spooked you, we'll get to the bottom of it."

"Hey, Penny's not the only one who has your back." Amelia leaned down so she was eye level with the serpent. "If you ever need help, Red and I are here for you too. Okay?"

Boots reached up to flick a tongue on Amelia's cheek as a sign of thanks. She curled into Penny's lap, then sniffed at the torn, bloodied shirt and coughed in disgust. Boots wriggled backward and made a show of rolling on the bed to clean herself.

"Hey!" Penny squealed. "I have to sleep on that!"

Chuckling, Amelia tossed Penny a towel. "You go shower, I'll stay here with the germophobic reptile."

Shooting Amelia a grin of gratitude, Penny grabbed some clothes. "Is that okay, Boots? I won't be long."

Boots gave an unimpressed sniff and turned away before slithering over to Amelia's bed.

Penny gave her a fond look. "I'll take that as a yes."

When she returned, the room was tidy, and Amelia had changed into fresh clothes. Boots was sprawled across Penny's bedspread, which she was pleased to see was still clean.

"Thanks, Amelia. I feel a thousand times better now." Penny's stomach protested that by growling loudly. "Or I will with some food in me."

Boots dropped off the bed and came to sit at Penny's feet.

"If I don't see you before you go tonight, be careful, okay?" Amelia asked. A slight frown creased her brow. "I don't feel great about someone trying to get into our room while Boots was alone."

"I don't either," Penny said. "I'll speak to the dean about it. This place is like Fort Knox. I'm sure there will be hallway cameras. Maybe we can find out who it was?"

When the two girls parted ways at the dining hall, most of Amelia's concerns seemed to be relieved. Still, she gave Penny's hand one last squeeze before she left. "Remember, be *careful.*"

"You too!" Penny shot back. "You never know what kind of weird Irish creeps might be hanging around after dark."

"Hey!" Red popped around a corner. "I resemble that remark." He pulled Amelia away. "Hurry up, love. The library closes at eight. That only gives you an hour to do your research."

"It's only ten past six," Amelia said, double-checking her watch.

"Aye. We'll need the rest of the time for canoodling." He winked, dodging the hand that tried to swat his head.

"You only need two and a half minutes for that," Amelia remarked pointedly.

Red clutched his chest and staggered back. "You wound me with your overly truthful accusations."

Penny shook her head at their antics as she waved goodbye and headed for the dining room. Even before she arrived, the aroma of rich pasta sauce hit her like a tsunami. Penny wasn't the only one with a growling stomach, it seemed. Even Boots got excited, scooting under several tables and almost tripping a student in her quest to secure herself a slice of lasagna.

Penny made for her usual table but veered left when she spotted a familiar face. She pulled out a chair beside Dean March.

"I'm so sorry to interrupt your meal," Penny began.

"Don't worry." The dean gestured to her own empty plate. "I've finished eating. I'm back on the clock, so to speak."

"Dean, are there security cameras in the second-floor hallways?" Penny scooped lasagna onto her fork and shoved it in her mouth, chewing quickly.

Dean March nodded. "Is this to do with Trevor's disappearance? Because you'll have to explain how the girl's dorms are linked to that."

Penny shook her head, then stopped. Could it be? "I'm

not sure," she admitted. "When I got back this afternoon, Boots had barricaded the door with a chair. She said someone tried to break in."

"Boots *said?*" The dean's laser focus turned to Boots.

"I asked a bunch of questions," Penny quickly explained. "And she nodded or shook her head. It's not perfect. I still don't know who it was or what they wanted."

"Boots, do you know the person who tried to enter the room?" Dean March asked the serpent directly.

Boots nodded.

"Was it a student?" When Boots indicated 'no", Dean March asked if it was a professor. She pursed her lips when Boots nodded. "Did they attempt to force their way in?"

Boots hesitated.

Dryly, Penny took point on the next question. "Boots, did someone knock at the door and scare you?" A nod. "But they *didn't* try to kick down the door. You just got spooked because someone came looking for Amelia or me?"

Boots shook her head, then nodded, then shook again.

"What does that mean?" Dean March whispered.

"I think she's confused." Penny eyed the snake, who bared her fangs at the accusation. "Or embarrassed."

Boots threw her head onto the table dramatically.

"Sorry, Dean." Penny blew on another forkful of food. "She's been a bit skittish lately."

"It's perfectly all right, dear." Dean March held a hand up to forestall any reply Penny might try to make while her mouth was full. "I'll have a look at that footage, just in case."

Boots lifted her head up and nodded eagerly.

"Take care, my dears." Dean March collected her plate and cutlery to return it to the kitchen.

Penny finally gulped down her food. "Dammit, Boots," she muttered. "You had me thinking someone was out to get you."

"Out to get who?" Cisco grinned at Penny as he flipped a chair around to sit on. "How was your trip to the abandoned lot, did you find anything?"

Penny groaned. "It was a bust. Well, I think it was. No sign of technologically advanced spy organizations, just an evil witch and a sight that almost blinded me, it was so horrific." Penny told him the story of Anna Marple, Perkins, and Red's torn pants. "I owe him a new pair of strides," she finished. "His were completely destroyed."

"I'm sure he doesn't mind," Cisco pointed out. "I mean, it was for Trevor, right?"

"Yeah. I know." Penny let out a slow breath. She was tired, aching, and stressed to the max over Trevor's disappearance. "Sorry, I'm such a buzz kill when I'm worried."

"Not at all!" Cisco grinned. "But as your boyfriend, it's my job to help you chill."

"You're my boyfriend now?" Penny teased. "After one date?" She had to admit, it was the *best* date she'd ever been on.

"Is that not how it works?" Cisco's eyes twinkled. "Then quick, let's have another one."

"What, now?" Penny chuckled as he nodded seriously.

"I even came prepared." Cisco fished in his pocket and pulled out a tiny battery operated tea light candle. "And you say I'm disorganized!"

Choking on a mouthful of food, Penny tried not to laugh. "Cisco, you're adorable."

"I know." He slid his plate a little closer to hers and set

his phone on the table. He pressed the screen a few times and tweaked the volume.

"What song is that?" Penny tilted her head to she could hear it better over the buzz of noise in the dining hall. "Is that… Is that the love song from *Lady and the Tramp*?"

"When the moon hits your eye," Cisco's deep baritone rang out through the room, loud and off-key. "Like a big pizza pie…"

Boots rolled herself off the table and hid behind Penny's feet.

I'm glad someone has that option, Penny thought.

With all eyes in the room now on him, Cisco grinned, stood, and bowed to the dining hall. He waved away his spectators. "The show's over, go back to your dinner."

Penny eyed him warily. "Do you have anything else planned?"

Cisco patted his pockets down and tipped his head to one side. "I'm sure I had a mariachi band in here somewhere." He shrugged. "I must have left it at home. That one will have to wait till next time."

Penny giggled, which made her blush, which made her laugh even harder. "Never a dull moment with you, is there?"

"I do my best." Sobering, Cisco changed topics. "But on a more serious note, what are we gonna do about Trevor?"

Penny wished the moment of peace had lasted just a little bit longer. "I've set up a seance at the Bagdad tonight, so I can question Tilly." When he squinted in confusion, she explained who Tilly was. "It was Paddy's idea, and DeLouise set it up for me."

"Anything I can do?" he asked.

Penny shrugged. "Is there anything you can think of? I have Paddy keeping an ear out. Esmerelda is going to ask around, too. Crenel is trying to organize a chat with those guys who were kidnapped. The only other thing I can think of is trying to find out who Trevor was working with, but I don't even know where to start!"

"Mom might know who Trevor has been hanging around with," Cisco suggested. "I'll ask her, and I'll talk to Professor Anand, too."

"Good idea." Penny sighed. "When this all done, though, I might need some counseling. Every time I close my eyes, I see the horrifying image of Red in his torn-up yoga pants."

Shuddering, Cisco pushed his now-empty plate away. "I'm glad I'm finished eating because you just killed what was left of my appetite."

"I just wish we had a definitive answer about that house. Did the spooks pull the address out of thin air? Or did they know about the witch, hell, did they put the witch there?" Penny tapped the table with her fingertips. "How many strings are these guys pulling?"

"We'll get them," Cisco told her confidently. "And we'll get Trevor home safely."

CHAPTER SEVENTEEN

Penny met Agent DeLouise outside the Bagdad Pub just after one AM the next morning. The restaurant had closed an hour ago, the tables long since cleaned down and the kitchen stripped and sterilized.

DeLouise led her inside, past a sleepy-looking waitress clutching a cluster of keys. "Thanks for staying." The agent spoke as if the young woman had a choice, rather than being ordered by her manager, who in turn was under instructions from the FBI.

"No problem." The sleepy waitress mustered a grin. "It's time-and-a-half for doing nothing."

DeLouise accompanied Penny to the atrium, then nodded toward the kitchen doors. "All yours, Penny. You want me to come with, or wait outside?"

"Outside is fine." Penny knew DeLouise would follow orders to do pretty much anything, but that didn't mean she was happy about attending the seance. Not only that, but Penny hadn't mentioned she was bringing a friend. She knew Boots wouldn't cause a health hazard in the kitchen, but having her there still might cause problems if anyone found out. "I'll try not to take too long."

Inside, Penny picked a spot on the floor to work. The stainless steel countertop would give her more space, but damned if she wasn't aching to sit down.

When she opened the bag, Boots slowly unfurled and stretched out, uncomfortable after being jammed up against Penny's other supplies.

"Remember, love, you're not supposed to be here," Penny reminded her in a whisper.

Boots gave a gentle hiss of assent and curled up quietly to watch. Penny unpacked her kit—a small folding table, a silk cloth, some candles, salt, a pen, and a notebook.

The few classes they'd had on summoning ghosts had been vague. Penny was instead relying on information gathered from her ghostly friends at Paddy's. One young specter had suggested that since the Veil tearing, pretty much any ceremony had a decent chance of working. All the more so if the entity in question wanted to make contact.

Penny spread the cloth over the table and arranged the candles in a star shape. She lit the candles before turning off the cold white lights overhead, then returned to the makeshift altar and sat before it with her legs crossed and palms up. She took five slow, deep breaths before beginning.

Something butted her leg, and she opened one eye. "Yes, Boots?"

Boots pointed her nose at one of the candles and tapped it with her snout. Penny eyed the table. Sure enough, the candle Boots had identified was just slightly out of alignment with the others.

"Thanks, lovely." Penny adjusted the five-pointed star and tugged a wrinkle out of the altar cloth. Satisfied, she closed her eyes again "I call on the ghosts of the Bagdad theatre. I call on the protectors and the helpers. I call on the ghosts of the Bagdad Theatre."

Penny repeated the chant until her posture relaxed and her ears buzzed. A warmth draped her shoulders, and the soft glow behind her eyelids flickered "Tilly, are you there? Please, I need your help."

Penny felt the presence before she heard the scritch of pen on paper. Her eyes snapped open, and she watched the floating pen painstakingly etch out an answer.

You came back?

Penny gave a self-conscious laugh. "Yes, I did."

The ghoul was banished from here. He is gone. Thanks to you. The pen dropped back to the table.

"That's not why I'm here." Penny took a deep breath. "I'm here for information, this time." She gave the listening ghost—ghosts?—a brief explanation of the arcade game, the mysterious entity behind it, and her missing friend. "I've asked around the Myther community," she finished. "They all said I'd need to talk to a local. So here I am."

The pen sat on the altar, unmoving. It twitched, then rose again.

You are working with the godmothers.

It wasn't a question but Penny nodded. "I asked one for help, yes. It's good to see she followed through with her promise."

We know of this entity you speak of. It is not spoken of, but we owe you a debt.

"Well, that goes both ways." Penny knew she might be giving away her only advantage, but she wasn't one to play an unfair hand. "When old cutthroat bailed us up in the kitchen, you guys saved our asses. I owe you for that."

The very edges of Penny's senses tingled and Boots gave a dry cough, a sound that usually signaled a chuckle. Penny narrowed her eyes at the serpent, but bit her tongue. She didn't want to interrupt her otherworldly conversation in case the ghosts disappeared completely.

The ones you seek exist in the shadows. That is their purpose, their identity. Only the brightest of lights will vanquish them. Do not leave them even a sliver of darkness to withdraw to.

"How do I find them?" Penny asked urgently.

You do not. The pen jostled, fell, and moved again as though two invisible hands fought over it. After a tense pause, it began to write again. *They know you seek them. They will find you. Be careful, Penny Hingston.*

The pen fell with a clatter, landing on the tiled floor as the candles snuffed out. Turning on a flashlight, she reread the final message the ghosts had left her. *They will find you.*

Penny shivered, goosebumps pricking at her arms. "Well. I guess *that* conversation is over."

Boots hissed and slithered over to her. She picked up the pen between delicate fangs and dropped it into the open knapsack.

Penny dismantled the tiny altar, wrapped the still-warm candles in the cloth, and packed everything away. She kept the notebook out, not wanting to risk any damage from warm candle wax.

"Come on, in you go." Penny held the bag open for Boots, who wriggled in and ducked her head so Penny could zip it up.

DeLouise jumped when Penny emerged.

"Sorry." Penny gave an embarrassed grin. "I didn't mean to scare you."

"Who said that I was scared?" DeLouise gave Penny a defiant glare, though there was a tell-tale twinkle in her eye. "Right?"

"Right." Penny gestured toward the front doors of the theatre. The waitress had leaned her back on one of the glass panels and was puffing away at a cigarette. "Shall we go?"

DeLouise nodded and started toward the exit. "Did you get what you needed?"

"Close enough," Penny answered. To be honest, she wasn't sure exactly how to interpret the information she had been given. She knew that the clandestine organization was very good at hiding. Shine the light? She didn't think the ghosts were being literal, though the image of their hidden compound being lit up by searchlights and broadcast all over the local news gave her a grim satisfaction.

They left the Baghdad side-by-side after DeLouise stopped for a quick word with the waitress. "You hungry?" The FBI agent asked as she unlocked the car. "I'd kill for a burger."

Penny shook her head. Staying up this late wreaked havoc with her metabolism. She was, in fact, starving, and her earlier use of the healing staff hadn't helped. Boots had twitched at the mention of food, though. Penny didn't want to risk the serpent revealing herself to the agent.

DeLouise chuckled. "It's okay, Boots. I know you're in there."

Boots shoved her nose out of the top of her bag, raising her head and hissing happily. Wincing, Penny asked the agent how she figured it out.

"You know those pregnant women that always have a hand on the stomach?" DeLouise pointed to Boots' hiding spot. "That's you and that bag. You haven't noticed how you wrap your arms around it and constantly pat it when Boots is inside?"

"I do not!" After a moment's consideration, Penny had to backtrack that statement. "Okay, but it's not *that* noticeable."

"It's my job to notice things." DeLouise rounded a corner, then pointed toward the glowing lights of a nearby diner. "Last chance."

Boots twisted and wiggled, freeing her tail so she could point in the direction of the offered food.

"We'd love to stop," Penny admitted dryly.

CHAPTER EIGHTEEN

Days passed. Penny was finally allowed access to the arcade machine, only to find the high scores had been wiped. The forensics team denied it was them, and Penny was inclined to believe them. Deleting a few pixels on a screen was surely easier than making that machine appear in the blink of an eye.

In fact, a new machine had appeared at Tony's the day after this one had been taken. The cafe owner had been dubious about keeping it, but Penny pointed out it was probably better to cordon it off, rather than risk yet another one popping up for some poor sap to use.

Crenel's contacts at the local police precincts finally came through, but Penny's interview with the two kidnapped men was a bust. Though both had been as helpful as they could, whatever their captors had done to them had wiped every memory of their time away, as well as the game itself.

Even Esmerelda had come up bust. A bluebird had swooped into the dining hall one morning, narrowly avoiding a curious nip from Boots. It dropped a tiny scroll in Penny's eggs and darted out the window.

I apologize for the delay, and for my lack of assistance. The information you seek is not known to those I associate with. I do hope you find the boy. —E.

And, the final blow to Penny's plans, she had made no progress in tracking down Trevor's mysterious partner. He hadn't kept a single written note in his room and his laptop and phone were locked down tight, with security that even the FBI task force hadn't been able to crack.

Unable to come up with any more leads, Penny had no choice but to wait for the day the organization was due to collect Tony's machines for servicing.

At each class, a professor would call Penny aside to ask if there was any news yet. Each time, it drove home the fact that there was nothing to do but wait. Lectures passed by in a blur, Penny's mind was too preoccupied to pay attention. Thankfully, her instructors were sympathetic to this fact. She ended the week with a fat stack of class notes to go over when she was in a better frame of mind.

The only professors who didn't give her any quarter were Glass and Steele.

Glass pushed her harder than ever. Penny didn't mind. The physical nature of his classes numbed her mind and worked her body to exhaustion. He insisted distraction was no excuse for sloppiness, and that out in the real world, this was something his students would simply have to learn to deal with.

Penny knew he was right. She welcomed the chance to hone her skills in preparation for the day when she would finally catch up with those who had taken her friend. She welcomed his brisk manner and lack of sympathy. After each fitness and defense lesson, she came out bone-weary and dripping with sweat, her mind finally too tired to focus on the needling anxiety she otherwise felt.

Though she welcomed Glass's strictness, Steele's rankled her. The New Zealander constantly prodded her with questions about Boots—her diet, her habits, her intelligence. More and more, Penny found herself holding back answers, especially regarding the extent to which Boots understood the world around her.

"You need to study her more thoroughly," Steele repeated for about the third time that lesson. "Your grades depend upon it."

Penny's irritation bubbled over. "I thought my grades depended on a thorough knowledge of myth and Legend across the Australasian regions. Not the shitting habits of my pet snake."

Steele's eyes narrowed, but she turned away. "Fine. We'll focus on Balinese archaeology instead."

Penny guessed that the topic was supposed to be a form of punishment. The history behind various ancient sculptures and statues was something she would normally find tedious. Today, she was just glad that the topic was no longer her friend.

When the final bell sounded for the evening, Penny didn't wait for her instructor's permission to pack up her things and leave. She slammed her books into her bag and stalked out without a goodbye.

She met Amelia in the dining room. "Thank God that's over."

Amelia passed Penny Boots' bag. "That bad?"

Penny peeked in the bag. Boots was either sleeping soundly or doing a really good job of pretending. She had asked Amelia to watch the serpent during her class since the idea of subjecting Boots to Steele's probing questions made her feel sick. "Thanks for watching her."

"It was hardly difficult." Amelia shoved her head into the bag and cooed. "You're such a precious girl, aren't you?"

Boots finally roused at this, sleepily emerging to flick a tongue at Amelia's nose.

"Suck up." Penny took the bag and headed for a table. "How are you going with that research?"

Amelia groaned and flopped into her seat with a dramatic flounce. "I hate research. Seriously, trawling these ancient message boards full of stuff I don't understand is a whole kind of hell in itself. I mean, there was this whole thing about camping! Cool, I thought, I love camping. But they weren't talking about camping, but some kind of cheat. Or maybe it was just a clever strategy, I don't really know." Amelia pulled a notebook out of her bag and tossed it toward Penny. "This is all I got on Polybius."

Penny flicked the cover open. The book was crammed with neat, tiny handwriting with occasional notes in the margin. A dozen pages in, however, and the rest was blank.

Rather than feel deflated, Penny mustered a grin. "It's better than nothing, and loads better than I could have done, mate."

"Don't get excited until you read it," Amelia warned. "The most interesting thing about the whole damn thing is that there *is* no information."

"I'm sure it's not *that* bad." Penny had read Amelia's class notes before and knew her friend was meticulous and concise.

"No, I mean it." Amelia drummed her fingers on the table. "Whoever this organization is, they're sneaky. Like, really sneaky. I mean, they've been operating for what, four or five months at least? Any other Myther event would have hundreds of posts online about it. This?" Amelia shook her head, solemn. "It's just not talked about, to the point where it's like the information has been wiped."

"How would you even know that?" Penny asked dubiously. *If information isn't there, it simply isn't there, right?*

Amelia opened the notebook and flicked through a few pages. She jabbed a finger at one entry. *HunterX: no log entries on relevant days.*

"Hunter posts daily, even if nothing new is going on. All the dates I looked up, the days those boys were both reported missing, the days they re-appeared—nothing. Nada, zilch, zero. That's a giant red flag, Penny."

"Maybe he was just busy?" Penny suggested. "Did you ask him?"

"Her," Amelia clarified. "I'm pretty sure it is, anyway. And yeah, I sent her an email." She fiddled with her phone, reflexively waking it up to check her notifications. "She hasn't responded yet."

"That's because email isn't safe." A small girl with black hair slammed a stack of folders on the dining table beside Penny. She lifted a pierced eyebrow and jutted her chin at Amelia. "Seriously, these guys are everywhere, tracking digital footprints and hacking into servers at the drop of a hat to delete information. Why on earth would you think your email is secure?" She tilted her head up and regarded

Amelia through narrowed eyes. "What's your interest in *Polybius*, anyway?"

Penny opened her mouth to answer but Amelia got in first.

"*You're* Hunter X? Little Jessie Grey is *Hunter X*?" Amelia hastily wiped her grin away when the girl scowled.

Jessie folded her arms and lifted her eyebrows haughtily. "Yeah? So what if I am?"

Amelia pulled a chair out and gestured for the girl to sit. "If you are, we're in the company of greatness. Hunter X is *the* online source for all things Myther. No one else is better at sniffing out a mystery or busting a hoax." She glanced around, then leaned closer. "How'd you get in here? If you get caught sneaking into this academy, they'll—"

Jessie snorted. "I'm a *student*, thank you. Cybermyth track."

"I haven't seen you in Prof Anand's class," Penny pointed out. "What year are you?"

"First." Jessie grimaced. "They won't actually let me *take* Cyber until third semester, but I've already got my name down. Trevor was sneaking me notes so I could get a head start on the class. In return, I agreed to help him with his case."

Penny's stomach dropped. "You said 'was.'"

Rolling her eyes, Jessie slapped a hand on the files. "Duh. He disappeared. Taken by those goons who kidnapped the other two geeks, only they haven't brought Trevor back."

"But why?" Penny demanded. "Why not drop Trevor back with a bit of mind voodoo?"

"Because he knows too much. And because the three weeks aren't up. That's probably relevant." Jessie leaned forward in her seat. "Look, I know I'm not as old as you guys, or as pretty or cool." Somehow the look on her face suggested she thought she was actually quite a bit more "pretty and cool" than Penny and Amelia. "And I'm not trained to go out in the field yet. But Trevor was my friend, and he knew something was up with that game. He linked me all the rumors that started in the eighties, and it gets *so much weirder.*"

She waited for Penny and Amelia to ask before continuing. "Every time I post about it on my boards, the posts disappear a few hours later. There were the two disappearances, and now Trevor..." Her voice dropped to a whisper. "Whoever these guys are, they're *smart.*" Jessie's eyes darted around and she stood. "The green folder is the one you want," she hissed, then added loudly. "Like, yeah, girls. We should totally party this weekend." Rolling her eyes, she stalked off.

"Who... What?" Penny watched her go, trying not to let her jaw hang open.

"I used to babysit that kid," Amelia told Penny. "She hasn't changed a bit."

"You babysat her?" Penny asked.

Amelia nodded. "She'd probably kill me if she knew I told you, but yeah. She lived at the other end of my street. Her mom was worried her tiny little goth baby wasn't 'integrating into society' enough so she would pay me to watch her after school."

"I bet that was a blast." Penny reached for the green folder. "Did she always have so much attitude?"

Amelia chortled. "No. She probably got it off me, in fact. I'm the one who taught her how to apply that eyeliner and how to stand up to her mom."

"Oh." Penny tipped her head to one side, thinking. "How old is she?"

"There are four years between us," Amelia explained.

"So, almost eighteen?"

Penny raised her eyebrows. *Eighteen, and Crenel told me they only take the best, the ones with a bit of life experience.* "If the Academy brought Jessie in at such a young age, she must have been an outstanding candidate."

"That, or she blackmailed them." Amelia didn't seem to be joking. "But hey, she's given us a bunch of information. Maybe it'll help us to find Trevor."

Penny skipped classes the next day. She holed up in her room with Boots and Amelia, combing through Jessie's stack of research. It contained lists of arcade machine appearances, dates of disappearances and reappearances, and the address Penny had visited with Red and Amelia. That had been circled in red pen with a post-it note stuck on top that said 'likely trap.' Penny snorted at that, then crossed out "likely" and penciled in "definitely."

It seemed the goons always traveled in pairs and drove nondescript black SUVs. They would always arrive to collect the machine data on schedule, and the money was always left with the owner of the location.

Penny learned that both men who had been kidnapped had interacted with the goons. The younger one who'd disappeared from the pool had argued with one when he was in the middle of a game. They had wanted to "run their update" and clean out the cash box, but he'd insisted on finishing his turn. When they offered him a handful of quarters as "compensation," he had refused. That day, the goons had simply walked out, climbed in their van, and, according to the dashcam footage of a car that had driven past, radioed someone before driving off.

"How did she even get access to this stuff?" Penny asked. "Let alone track it down in the first place."

"When she was six, she rigged up her nanny-cam to a looping still so she could sneak into the kitchen and raid the snacks," Amelia told her proudly. "This was probably a piece of cake."

What Jessie hadn't figured out—and what Penny needed to know most—was where the hell they came from. The vans, the machines… All of it must be stored in a location, and that location was more than likely where they were holding Trevor.

"There's just one more thing to try," Penny muttered.

"You're gonna do something really dumb, aren't you?" Amelia asked.

Penny shrugged one shoulder. "Is it really that dumb if it works?"

CHAPTER NINETEEN

Penny leaned forward to peek around the corner. "There they are!"

Cisco tossed her a helmet and started his bike engine. "Let's go."

The low rumble made Penny wince, but she threw a leg over the bike and wrapped her arms around Cisco's waist. The bike rolled forward smoothly, out of the alley and into the street. Cisco faced the bike away from Tony's coffee shop, parking it two spaces behind the shiny black SUV instead. Two men were just yanking the front doors open to get into the van.

"You don't think we're a little close?" Penny asked him. "This is supposed to be a stealth mission."

"Best place to hide is in plain sight," Cisco told her. "Don't worry. I'll put some distance between us when they go."

Ahead, the van's brake lights glowed, then dimmed as it pulled out into the traffic beside them. Cisco waited for a few cars to pass, then did the same.

"Don't lose them." Despite her concerns that they were too close just moments ago, Penny couldn't help feeling a flare of worry that they would lose their mark. If they did, it would be seven whole days before they'd have another chance.

Cisco nodded, carefully turning into a side lane after the van. He let another car pass at the next corner, but two more peeled away at an intersection, leaving only a garbage truck between the two students and their quarry.

The van picked up speed while the truck lagged behind on the small incline. Then, brake lights glowed as the truck came to a sensible halt at a traffic light that had just turned yellow.

"Shit!" Penny cursed their bad luck. "They're turning. We're going to lose them!"

Cisco shook his head and waited patiently for the light to turn green. As soon as it did, he took off, zooming into the turning lane beside them. He wove through traffic, taking a left, then a hard right.

Penny's head spun but she clung tight to Cisco, trusting him to find his way through the narrow streets and heavy traffic.

"Ha!" The bike stopped abruptly at a red light, and Cisco tapped the side mirror. Penny craned her head over his shoulder to look. The van was behind them, yellow indicator flashing steadily on the left.

Cisco took the corner and the van followed. When it took a second turn, this time without the telltale signal, he almost missed it. "I think they've seen us," he called over the engine. "Time for a costume change."

He swung the bike around and onto the sidewalk. He

kicked out the stand and tore off his helmet and jacket. "The street they took comes around this way. If we run through the park, we should be able to catch them."

Penny shed her black jacket to reveal a hot pink crop and grabbed one of the skateboards off the bike. She shook out her hair to complete the transformation. To a casual passerby, the two helmeted, black-clad bikers had no resemblance to the brightly dressed skateboarders who sprinted through the tiny green space in the middle of Portland.

"Let's go!" On the other side of the park, Penny threw her board down and jumped on, crouching low to keep her balance. The van slipped into a side street ahead. She reached into a pocket and depressed the small remote to bring the board—a high-tech electric version capable of matching the traffic around them—up to full speed. Penny gave mental thanks to Mack, who had not only provided the skateboards but spent the morning making sure Penny and Cisco could use them capably.

Penny dodged a cluster of pedestrians, taking a driveway onto the road before racing across it. She flicked the end of the board up, skidding to a halt as Cisco caught up. "That way!" she called. The van was directly ahead, trundling toward an industrial estate. "We're not gonna have a lot of cover down there."

"You think?" Cisco pointed at a group of five teenagers flipping boards outside an abandoned building. One tossed a ball of wadded paper at the van as it passed and it bounced off, rolling into the gutter. "We'll be fine."

"Sure." Penny eyed the group. All wore dirty black jeans and monochrome t-shirts. "We'll totally blend in."

Tugging her vibrant top down self-consciously, she kicked off again using foot power to propel the skateboard down the broken pavement. The van slowed, and without indicating this time it turned into a gated driveway. Outside, one of two armed guards barked orders into a radio.

Penny casually rode past, watching the slow metal panel pull back. The guards ignored her, focusing instead on the vehicle. She pretended to stumble and trip off the front of the skateboard, and slowly dusted herself off when she'd recovered her footing.

The building loomed over the worn and dusty factories and warehouses around it, standing tall and sharp-edged with expansive mirrored windows cladding the exterior. The compound was surrounded by concrete walls that obfuscated the lower floors, except for Penny's glimpse as the van rolled through the gate.

Penny stepped back on her board and cruised past, her need for secrecy overriding her desire for a closer look. She had glimpsed several black military-style vehicles and a row of identical white vans inside, but little of the ground floor of the building itself.

"That place is locked down tighter than a leprechaun's wallet." Cisco gestured for Penny to keep moving. "And I spotted at least four security cameras pointing at that gate as we went past."

"Did you see all those guards inside?" she whispered back. "At least a half dozen right at the gates, and a few more scattered near the building. Cisco, how the hell are we going to sneak past them?"

"We?" Cisco shook his head. "You're kidding, right? We can't do this ourselves."

The sudden realization that their job was over made Penny's knees weak with relief. *Of course.* She yanked her phone out and called Agent Crenel.

Penny tapped her foot nervously. The chain of black FBI vehicles had passed them at least five minutes ago. "Where *is* he?"

"He'll be here," Cisco assured her confidently.

Crenel had been very clear on his instructions to Penny. "At least three blocks away. I don't want you anywhere near that place when SWAT gets there, understand? I'll pick you up on the way."

Finally, one last black car came cruising around the corner and stopped in front of Penny and Cisco. A door flew open and Crenel barked, "In. Now."

Penny didn't wait to be told twice. She jumped in the car and slid across the back seat to make room for Cisco. "Have they found Trevor yet?" she asked eagerly.

Crenel didn't respond for a moment. When he did, it was in a hard and angry voice. "You kids better have a damn good explanation for leading us on this wild goose chase."

"Wild… what?" Penny looked at Cisco, who shrugged. "You mean Trevor wasn't there?"

"Where?" Crenel snapped. "In that empty paddock?"

Penny let out a growl of frustration. "You got the wrong address? How? You track my phone, for crying out loud!"

"Don't you try and weasel out of this one," Crenel told her. "My team went to your exact location. Which, yes, matched up to the address you left me."

Penny pressed a hand against the window. "Why the hell are you driving back to the Academy?"

"Where the hell else do you expect me to take you?" Crenel yelled, his anger finally getting the better of him. "Goddammit, Penny, this wasn't funny. It's an incredible waste of government resources, resources we could have been using to find Trevor."

"What are you talking about?" Penny yelled back. "We followed the van to that compound and called you right away! Why aren't you going there? Those are the guys that have Trevor, I swear!"

Crenel yanked on the steering wheel, cutting across a lane of traffic to turn the car around. The car lurched forward as he accelerated. "You wanna go there? We'll go there. Have your damn laughs."

Crenel took the same route Penny and Cisco had when following the mysterious white van that had picked up the arcade machine from Tony's. They passed the emo skater kids and slowed to a halt some way down the road.

"What? I don't get it." Penny could feel the tremor in her voice as she clutched at the door handle. She yanked it back and stumbled out of the car. "Cisco? This can't be happening."

She faced a vast, empty lot. No concrete walls or metal gates, no big glass building, and sure as hell no guys with machine guns waiting for them. "This… This isn't right! It was here. Minutes ago!"

"You expect me to believe that?" Crenel growled. He

seemed less certain in the face of Penny's reaction. "Listen, kid. I don't care what you do on your time off, but you haven't, you know…" He mimed a puff on an invisible cigarette.

Penny gave him a withering glare. "Fuck *you*. It was here." She stared at the lot a moment longer, then rounded on the agent. "Goddammit! If you hadn't told me not to stop and take pictures, I'd be able to prove it to you."

"He said that?" Cisco asked.

"It was for your own safety!" Crenel huffed a breath then pulled out a cigarette. "I didn't know you were just delusional."

"There was a building here," Cisco insisted. "And I can prove it." He fumbled his phone out.

"You took pictures?" Penny breathed.

Cisco shrugged. "You didn't tell me the old man said not to."

For a change, Crenel ignored the "old man" jab. He snatched Cisco's phone away from him and held it up. "This peak here is that old warehouse?" he asked.

Cisco squinted at the phone and nudged it to the left. "Yeah. There." The glowing image on the screen lined up perfectly with the surrounding buildings. It was just the one in the middle that had…vanished.

"I must be losing my mind." Penny pressed a hand to her head. "This… They made a *whole building* disappear?"

Crenel scowled at the vacant lot as if he could summon the compound back from force of will alone. "Impossible."

"Agent Crenel, my best friend sprouts fur and four legs every full moon," Cisco pointed out. "Missing buildings? Not so farfetched."

Crenel grunted but didn't respond.

Penny paced toward the lot. She stepped off the footpath, one hand out. She griped, searching for an invisible barrier.

"Don't bother," Crenel told her. "My people searched the lot top to bottom. No invisible walls, no secret underground passages. Whatever was here, it isn't anymore."

Penny persisted, reluctant to give in to the obvious fact that the building had indeed vanished. *If it was ever even here to begin with.* Below her feet, a thick layer of gravel was undisturbed.

"What if it was just an illusion?" Penny asked. "A hologram or something?"

Cisco hissed a breath through his teeth. "Nope. Remember the kid who threw a ball of paper at it? It bounced off."

Penny remembered and took off jogging down the street, leaving Crenel and Cisco to scramble to keep up with her. She found the paper napkin, still lying in the gutter. She unwrapped it, hoping for some kind of clue.

"Ew." Cisco sniffed it. "Oh, it's only melted chocolate. Mmm, peanut butter cups."

"This is real," Penny protested. "And the van was, too." She pointed back down the road. "I know that building was here. I saw those men walking around, Cisco. They had guns and cars and a big old building. You can't convince me it was fake."

"I'm not trying to," Cisco told her. "Look, we're dealing with myth and legend here. Anything is possible. For all we know, the whole place just folded up small enough to fit in a matchbox, and some guy walked away with it in his pocket."

"You watch too many movies, kid." Crenel finally lit his cigarette and drew on it deeply. He puffed out a cloud of smoke. "Let's get out of here. I'll put this place under surveillance for now."

"So you believe us?" Penny asked. She held her breath while she waited for an answer.

Crenel grimaced. "Yeah. I guess I never really thought you'd pull a stunt like that."

Penny socked him in the shoulder. "What the hell, dude!"

Crenel rubbed his arm and gave her a penitent wince. "I was pissed off. Trevor is still missing, and every damn time we get a lead, it vanishes into smoke and mirrors."

"Lead?" Penny stepped closer, pinning the agent against the car. "What lead?"

Crenel crumbled. "Fine! We've had three teams working this case. Yours, and two of ours. One of the teams emailed the boss to say they've found the compound. They went radio silent for three days, then turned up at the airport, memories wiped. They didn't remember a single damn thing about the mission they'd gone on."

"The other?" Penny pressed.

"The other lost one man in a shootout, and one of the women got brainwashed by one of those damn arcade machines. It turned up in her house, according to her husband, and she hasn't been the same since." Crenel inhaled deeply on his cigarette again. "I know, I should have told you. I didn't wanna scare you off. You're our best chance, going by how badly the rest of them screwed up."

"Crap on a cracker." Penny rubbed her hands over her face. "You really think we can do better than seasoned agents?"

"Are *you* dumb enough to actually play one of those machines?" Crenel shot back. "Do you have Kevlar under that shirt?"

"No, and yes." Penny lifted the edge of her t-shirt to reveal the armor beneath it. "But really. We don't exactly have a ton of field experience here."

"Which is why I had two backup teams, and yet this is the closest we've come to nailing these bastards down." Crenel pointed to the car. "Come on. Let's get you back to the Academy. We need a new plan."

CHAPTER TWENTY

After four hours of brainstorming, Crenel finally called a break. "We're all tired and hungry, and to be honest, I'm getting pissed off."

"Hungry is right." Agent DeLouise had joined them in Crenel's office at the Academy with a latte in one hand and a chicken sandwich in the other. She hadn't made a fuss when Crenel plucked it out of her hands and ate it, but now she rubbed her stomach.

"It's taco night in the dining hall," Penny told her. "Cook should nearly have it ready."

DeLouise shook her head. "I need to get back to the office." She jabbed a finger at Crenel. "And you need to come with me. There's no way they're gonna believe this whole vanishing building schtick without a firsthand witness."

"But I didn't witness it," Crenel pointed out.

DeLouise flicked a glance at Penny. "You really want to pit a student against that asshole Banks? He'll tear her a new one."

"I can take him," Penny interjected immediately. "I know what we saw."

"It's fine." Crenel grabbed his sunglasses and wallet off his desk. "I'll go. Banks loves me."

"Damn right he does." DeLouise flashed Penny a grin before turning back to Crenel. "Once you get Banks off my ass, I can go hunt down that damn tooth fairy on the east side."

"Tooth fairy?" Penny asked. It hadn't come up in their weekly class briefing.

DeLouise rubbed a hand over her mouth absentmindedly. "Yeah. She's been breaking into houses at night and stealing kids' teeth."

"From under their pillows?" Penny asked, her stomach churning.

DeLouise shook her head.

"Spare me the details." Penny stood. "If you don't mind, I'm outta here. If I come up with anything I'll let you know, Agent Crenel."

"Sure, Penny." Crenel touched her shoulder as she passed him. "Don't worry. We'll find him."

Penny nodded briskly and walked out of the room, shoulders set and jaw clenched. She waited until she was around the corner to lean against a wall and let out a slow, shaky breath. *Come on, Trevor, where are you?*

She heard the agent's door close as she set off toward the dining hall, unwilling to wait for the agents to catch up to her and offer more platitudes. So far, their best—their *only* plan—was to wait until the following Wednesday and hope the arcade machine would be picked up again.

"Fat chance," Penny mumbled. Tony had already

informed them that the replacement machine hadn't turned up at its usual time.

Penny bypassed the dining hall and headed for the dorms. She was so buried in her thoughts she didn't see the girl coming from the other direction. Penny and Jessie plowed into each other.

"Oh, hell. Sorry, mate!" Penny grabbed Jessie's arm to steady her as the girl clutched the fat leather book she had almost dropped.

"No problem!" Jessie gave her a cheerful grin. She darted off but not before leaning into Penny for an awkward moment.

Penny watched her go, then slipped a hand into her pocket where Jessie had pressed against her. A tightly folded note brushed her fingers. "You sly thing."

Worried about the secrecy Jessie had employed to pass it on, Penny waited until she was in her room to open it.

Space Buster app is recording your calls and location, delete it. Also, your room is bugged. New machine at the Twisted Monkey biker bar, data pickup sometime tonight. Be careful.

Penny shot a quick glance at her watch. "I've got some time." Then she looked at her phone. "And what the hell?"

Penny opened the app menu and scrolled through. Sure enough, a tiny icon for 'Space Busters' sat nestled between Settings and Spotify. Penny held down the icon and slid it over to the delete option, then restarted her phone. *Good, it's still gone.*

Penny sank onto her bed, then stood as a spike heel stabbed her thigh. "Amelia! Dammit, this room was spotless a few days ago!"

Clothes were strewn across the room, and an empty suitcase sat ajar at the foot of Amelia's bed. An open bedside drawer was full of makeup, and the wardrobe had a pile of shoes in front of it.

Penny called for Boots. The room was silent. "Guess you don't like the mess either," Penny muttered as she searched for the supposed bug.

She found one under her bedside table, crushed it under her heel, and kept looking. She turned up four, by which point she was certain she had searched every square inch of the room. *And I still don't trust that I got them all.*

Resolving to have Crenel ask a team to do a sweep, Penny headed back into the hallway and locked her room behind her. Amelia was nowhere to be seen, so she made for Crenel's office. It was empty, the agents having already left to face the music from their superior.

"Guess we're on our own, then." She didn't want to consider the fact that she might not find any of her friends in time to intercept the arcade machine, that *she* might be on *her* own. "Professor Steele!" Penny called down the hall, spying the familiar face just before the professor disappeared around a corner.

The professor froze, clutching her tattered briefcase. "What?"

"Have you seen Cisco? Or Amelia and Red?"

Steele hesitated, then gave a jerky shake of her head. "I haven't seen the FBI agent, and I don't know who those other people are. I have to go."

"Where?" The question popped out before Penny could consider whether it was appropriate.

"None of your business." Steele swallowed, then spoke

again. "I have to return home. It's a family matter. Class this week is canceled."

She darted away, leaving Penny alone in the hallway. "That was just plain weird." Still, she didn't have time to worry about it.

In the short time since she had passed the dining hall, it had begun to fill with students eager for taco night. Heart thumping, Penny scanned the room.

"Cisco!" She waved a hand to catch his attention and gestured frantically for him to come over. When he was close enough, she leaned up to whisper loudly in his ear. "We have to go. I have a lead."

Cisco immediately went for his phone but Penny grabbed it, shaking her head wildly. "We were hacked. We can't call *anyone* until we check their phones." Sure enough, the Space Busters icon appeared on Cisco's phone as well. Penny deleted it. "That should fix it, I hope. Do you know where Amelia and Red are?"

Cisco shook his head. "Date night, I think."

"That explains the mess." Amelia had a habit of digging through her wardrobe like a drunk archaeologist in an Egyptian sandpit when she needed a date-night dress. "We'll have to go without them. Do you know where the Twisted Monkey is?"

Cisco coughed. "The Twisted… Are you sure?"

Penny passed him Jessie's crumpled note. "I trust my source."

"Oh. Right." With a weak smile, Cisco nodded toward the door. "Let's go, then. To the biker bar…"

The Twisted Monkey sat between a laundromat and a tattoo parlor. The signage for the tiny complex was worn and rusted, and the yellow light bulbs that lit the entrance to the bar buzzed when they flickered to life as Penny and Cisco approached. Above the door, a faded sign sporting a stylized monkey image tickled Penny's memory, but she was unable to place it.

Inside, the smell of stale beer and old cigarette smoke stung Penny's nose. She tried not to let it show, unwilling to display even a hint of weakness in front of the burly, bearded man at the bar, or the three guys in leather jackets in front of him.

"Look, boys." The bartender dropped a dirty cloth on the bar and gave a leering, gap-toothed grin. "We've got tourists."

The three patrons swiveled around to look at the newcomers. Penny resisted the urge to squirm under their scrutiny.

"Hi!" She gave a quick wave with the tips of her fingers. "We were just, um, in the area. Thought we'd drop by and grab a—"

"Members only." The bartender jerked his chin at the door.

"Wait on, Gus." One man stood and sauntered closer to Penny and Cisco. He leaned down until his face was only inches from Penny's. The cloying smell of sweat and rum made her stomach roil. Then, he grinned. "Hey! I know you."

"You… do?" Penny stared back, unable to dredge up any memory of the man.

"Yeah. You were at that meeting with all the weirdos,

right?" The man pointed at Penny, turning to his friends. "I saw her when I dropped Howler off."

A rush of relief flooded Penny as she realized why the monkey image out front had twigged her brain. "You're friends with Howler?" The Mayan Monkey God had only been into Paddy's a few times, but she knew he was one of the key players in the alliance.

The atmosphere suddenly eased, and Gus grabbed two glass steins and thumped them onto the counter. "What'll it be, ladies?"

Cisco coughed a rough laugh. "Thanks, but we're here on business."

"Oh?" Gus stepped back, suddenly guarded again. "Howler only does business by appointment."

Penny shook her head. "Not with him. We're here for that." She pointed at a dark corner of the bar where an arcade machine was nestled in the shadows.

"What's that?" One of the men squinted, then brightened. "Hey! When did we get pinball?"

He stood, but Penny jumped forward. "Mate, you do *not* want to play that."

"Who the fuck are you?" he asked, scowling at Penny. She met his narrowed eyes with confidence. "And why the hell not?"

"Because it's a government conspiracy." That shut the man down. He sat back on his barstool with a thump. "Not a real one. The men who put it here are Mythers. They've been kidnapping players and wiping their minds."

"Not much to wipe there," the bartender cackled.

"Hey, fuck you, Gus."

The bartender pulled his lips back in a chuckle. "Blow

me, Charlie." He shoved a fresh drink at the man, then looked back at Penny. "What's the story, then? You here to brainwash us?"

"We want to find the people behind this," Penny explained. "They took our friend."

"I can't help." Gus shrugged, though he looked upset that he couldn't help. "They didn't exactly give me a shipping address."

"It's okay." Penny motioned toward a seat in the corner. "Mind if we hang around for a while? My intel says it's being picked up tonight."

Gus pursed his lips. "I'll have to check with Howler. He's in charge when the boss is out." He tossed the rag down and left, vanishing behind an oaken office door.

Cisco gave Penny a nervous glance.

Gus re-appeared with a grin and motioned for them to accompany him into the office. "Howler says it's fine. You can hang around in his room while you wait. You can see everything from there."

Cisco trailed behind Penny, and she reached an arm back to clasp his hand. They passed the three drinking bikers and stepped into the office.

A steel desk in one corner propped up a cluster of small TV screens, each showing a different view of the bar and its surroundings. In the other corner, a large simian creature reclined in an armchair, a whittling knife in one hand and a block of wood in the other.

"Hey, Howler." Penny greeted the monkey god, not expecting a response. The Myther had been solemn and non-communicative the few times she'd seen him at

Paddy's, though the leprechaun had assured her it was simply his personality.

To Penny's surprise, Howler looked up and gave her a wide, toothy grin. He pointed to one of the screens, and Penny saw it was the one that showed the arcade machine. She leaned closer.

Cisco joined her, one hand on Penny's back for balance. "Am I the only one thinking we really need a plan here?"

Penny bit her lip, still watching the screen. "We follow the goons home, bust in, and steal Trevor back. That's a plan, right?"

"Ha." Cisco snorted. "Sure."

"They're a secret agency that can disappear on a whim. They made a whole damn office block vanish!" Penny blew out a frustrated breath. "If they're supposedly government, they're probably armed to the teeth."

"Even the government has weaknesses," Cisco pointed out. "Think, Penny. How many movies and urban legends are there of people sneaking into Area 51 or other secret bases?"

"A few," Penny admitted.

"So there's probably a way in." Cisco tapped the screen. "The very fact that there were stories about them in the first place means they were never believed to be completely invincible."

"Good point." Penny stood but didn't take her eyes off the screen. "I have an idea. Stand watch for a moment?"

They swapped positions, Cisco leaning one hip against the desk with his eyes locked on the surveillance screen while Penny dug around for her phone.

Hey Amelia, does your new blog have a video channel?

Her phone rang a few seconds later.

"Of course! You know I love that shit. Why? You want the link?" Amelia took a breath, but Penny cut her off.

"No, I want the logon. I swear, it's important, or I wouldn't ask." Penny held her breath for a beat. *Please don't ask questions.*

"Sure, I guess." Amelia sounded curious but thankfully didn't press for answers. A low chuckle nearby suggested she was otherwise occupied and Penny thanked her lucky stars. "It's just my regular email address as the login. The password is K9LOVR5861."

Penny snorted a laugh. "Really? K9LOVR? That's gold."

"What's yours?" Amelia shot back. "LatinoHottie123? Oh, hey, while I remember, I love you, girl but can you not trash our room like that without warning? Red came over and I nearly died!"

Penny's heart skipped a beat. "That wasn't you?"

"Me?" Amelia squealed. "Stop it, Red, this is important! No way. I left this room spick and span."

"Where is Boots?" Penny demanded.

"Boots?" All traces of laughter left Amelia's voice. "I thought she was with you. Penny, if you didn't make this mess…"

"Someone broke in," Penny finished. "Dammit! I knew Steele was acting shifty."

"Penny!" Cisco's hiss grabbed her attention. Penny saw two large shadows near the arcade machine, just out of the line of sight of the camera.

This is our only chance to get Trevor. But I can't leave Boots!

"Shit!" Penny's heart tore. "Goddamn it. Amelia, I need to call you back in a second. Don't go anywhere, okay?" Penny pressed the end call button, her movements weighed down by a heavy blanket of guilt.

Behind her, Howler shuffled to his feet and tapped Penny on the shoulder. He passed her the block of wood.

"Um, thanks?" Penny turned it over and blinked. "Wait, that's me!"

The monkey god had carved her likeness into one side of the block, depicting Penny standing tall with a sword in one hand and a rose in the other. Petals floated away from the dying rose, carved with such precision they looked as soft as silk.

Penny stared at her own face, the sculpture staring back with a hard expression.

"The rose is a symbol of secrecy," Penny whispered. "The secret organization. You mean, I should go after Trevor?"

Howler nodded.

"Will Boots be okay if I do?" she asked.

Penny waved off Cisco's questions with a hand as Howler nodded again.

Penny didn't hesitate. She called Amelia back and cut her friend off before she spoke. "Amelia? I need your help. I can't tell you what I'm doing, but I have to go."

"What?" Amelia snapped. "If Boots is—"

"If she is, I need you to find her for me." Penny clenched her jaw. "Please. You know how much she means to me. You know I would go to her if I had a choice."

"Okay." Amelia's voice changed from stunned to compassionate in a heartbeat. "I trust you, Penny. And you can trust me. You do what you need to do, and don't worry about Boots. I've got this."

Penny tapped the end call button. Cisco grabbed her arm. "What happened? You're white as a sheet."

She shook him off. "Nothing we can fix right now."

"Then let's go." The surveillance screen showed two suited men loading the arcade machine onto a dolly to wheel it out of the bar. Penny cracked the office door open and slipped out as they left. "Thanks for the help, guys."

"Bye!" Gus waved them off. "When you get the bastards, shoot them a few times for me!"

"Will do!" Penny ran to the door, paused, then followed the goons outside. The soft evening light cast long, deep shadows perfect for hiding. She passed Cisco a tiny adhesive tracking device. "Do it."

Cisco waited until the goons slammed the back door of the van shut and hauled themselves into the front. He darted across the alley they'd parked in and ran a hand softly along the bumper. He rolled behind a dumpster on the other side and gave Penny a thumbs up.

Penny waited for the van to sputter to life and roll away before sprinting for the Jeep she and Cisco had borrowed from the college. She threw herself in behind the driver's seat. "Let's get the bastards."

CHAPTER TWENTY-ONE

W hether it was a trick of the light, the traffic headed to a football game, or plain, dumb luck, the drive went smoothly. The van crawled through the traffic several cars ahead, then pulled off on a side street. Penny idled around the corner, then followed at a distance, headlights off.

The van stayed tantalizingly out of sight, but Cisco rattled off directions from the GPS tracker, guiding Penny into an industrial estate on the opposite side of town to the compound they had discovered last time.

"This must be it," Penny whispered as they crawled past. The van had taken a right turn into a gated driveway.

The Jeep cruised past, and once they were out of sight, Penny pulled into a vacant parking lot, positioning the car behind an old picket fence.

Cisco eased his door shut and eyed the car. "They'll find it if they look," he told her.

"Then let's hope they don't." Penny shut her own door and grabbed her phone.

Paranoia in full force, she quickly scanned her apps for anything that shouldn't be there. "All normal," she muttered as she dialed a number. "Are you ready to bring the light?" she asked.

"Affirmative." Cisco's voice was cold.

"I have a plan, but I need your help to make it work." Penny shivered in the cool evening air as she waited for an answer.

"Of course," Cisco told her. "Just tell me what to do."

Penny rattled off a list of instructions as Cisco set up the laptop. He pulled up a satellite view of the area.

When Penny was done, he pointed at an area of flat concrete. "What's that?"

Penny reached over him to zoom in on the area. "Our target." She scrolled around the edges, swapping into street view for a better look. "Hello, beautiful."

"That's a sewer cap," Cisco countered. "That's not beautiful. It's gross."

"It's exactly what we need," Penny urged. "Come on. When you picture breaking into a secret base, what's the first thing that comes to mind?"

"Subterranean adventure." Cisco sighed in defeat. "Let's hope it's as clean as it is in the movies. But if we meet any giant turtles down there, I'm out."

"Even if we did, they'd be on our side." Penny popped the trunk and started hauling out gear. "Headlamp?" She passed one to Cisco. "Body cams, pistols, smoke grenades. Oh, where are the signal jammers?"

"In that box." Cisco clipped a small glass hammer to his belt, then looped a length of rope around his middle. "Pity we don't have gumboots in here." He shuddered.

"You're such a girl," Penny told him.

"Really?" Cisco shot back. "You're really okay with traipsing through poop?"

"To get Trevor out?" Penny asked quietly. "Yeah."

"Of course I'll do it," Cisco hurriedly backed up. "But damned if I'm not gonna complain the whole way."

"Fair enough." Once she had all her gear, Penny locked the Jeep and tossed the keys under a wheel well. "That drain was around the east side of the building. Let's go."

They easily found the heavy metal plate covering a drain beneath the street. Cisco used a grappling hook to lift it and gestured for Penny to go first. "Let me know if I need to bag my feet," he called as she shimmied down the iron rungs.

"It's actually not too bad." Though a thin stream of water ran down the center of the tunnel, the smooth concrete walls were clean. A narrow ledge ran along the tunnel, toward an intersection that branched off in two opposing directions.

"Go left," Penny instructed after a glance at her phone.

They hurried through the tunnels until Penny pointed up. "Right here," she whispered. "We're about forty feet inside the boundary."

"What if it's swarming with gun-toting agents?" Cisco asked.

Penny shrugged. "Then we deal with that when we get there."

Ignoring Cisco's protest, Penny went up first. She climbed the steps embedded into the vertical tunnel and switched her headlamp off when she got to the top. As carefully as she could, she lifted the drain cover, looked around, then let it drop.

"We're in a loading bay," she whispered down to Cisco. "Looks empty."

"Great," Cisco muttered. "It *looks* empty."

Penny lifted the cap again and crept out, sliding the cover over to one side so Cisco could follow.

The section of the complex they had emerged in was clearly where the game machines were brought in. A row of white vans was parked against the building, and another van was parked with its back to an open loading dock.

Cisco re-covered their entry point as Penny kept watch.

The headlights of the van parked at the dock flashed twice. "Take cover!" Penny hissed.

The two friends dashed for the row of vacant vans. Penny peered through a tinted window as two heavyset men strode out from a loading dock door and climbed into the van.

"You want *how* many tacos?" one called.

"Nineteen altogether." A third man stepped out of the doorway, letting it swing shut behind him. "Gary said to remember his extra jalapenos. Moses forgot last time, and he was pissed."

"Whatever." The van doors slammed shut and the engine started.

Penny watched it drive away. A moment later, she heard the buzz of distant voices. *He must be talking to the guards at the gate.*

The man at the door touched his belt, then cursed. He lifted a large, box-shaped radio to his face and pressed a button. "Yo, Mike. Can you let me back in? I left my ID on the table."

After a brief moment of static, Mike answered. "I'm on the other side! You'll have to come in through the big door. Jesus, Bert. You're hopeless."

The roller shutter door beeped and slowly began to rattle up into the cavity above. Bert didn't wait for it to hit the top, ducking under it instead and disappearing around the corner. As soon as the bottom of the door reached the ceiling, it began its slow descent back down.

"Can you make it?" Penny whispered.

"Can't you?" Cisco teased.

The two bolted from their hiding place and sprinted across the loading dock. They came to a panting halt outside the door when it was still two feet from the ground. Penny dropped to her stomach to look inside, then flicked a hand signal at Cisco before rolling under it.

She sprang to her feet in time to see the door graze Cisco's hip as he slipped under. She motioned him to be silent, then pointed at a narrow hallway to one side. *Enemy that way,* she mouthed.

"*Go that way,*" Cisco responded.

Penny nodded. The guys in charge of loading the corrupted game machines were unlikely to hold notable positions in whatever this organization called itself.

They crept away from the low hum of voices, toward a corridor lit with bright, white fluorescent bulbs that reflected off the white tile floor. Penny walked fast, her gun trained at the corner ahead. When voices approached she held up a hand, but Cisco had already halted.

Penny pressed against the wall, a length of wire dangling from one hand.

Two men walked around the corner side by side, lost in conversation. "I swear to God, if they're using the vans for a taco run again—"

Penny sprang, looping her garotte around the closest man's throat before he had time to react. He clutched his neck but she tightened her grip, ignoring the strained gurgling sounds he made as he struggled.

Next to her, Cisco stood back as the man he'd taken down slumped to the floor, his neck broken.

"I wish I was better at that," Penny murmured.

"You do just fine without it." Cisco gestured to the man in her arms. He'd stopped struggling a few moments earlier.

She let him fall to the ground and began searching his pockets. "Ha! What's a secret agency without magic ID cards, eh?"

Cisco grinned and plucked a similar plastic square from the body at his feet. "Let's hope these do the trick."

He made to leave, but Penny yanked his arm back and motioned to a nearby door. "Ugh. You boys are such slobs! Are you gonna help me clean up this mess, or what?"

Penny dragged the body over to the door. The handle didn't budge when she tried it, but when she flicked the stolen ID near a small black box beside the jam, it beeped, and a green light flashed. "I'll hold the door."

Cisco stuck his tongue out at her but pulled the men one by one into the room. He stood and stretched. "Someone needs to skip taco night, that's for sure."

"Let's go." Penny let the door swing shut and watched as

the green light changed to red. "Hopefully, no one misses those guys for a while."

The hallway linked to a labyrinth of winding corridors. Twice they avoided notice by slipping into vacant rooms and once by simply shooting the three guards that appeared out of nowhere. Just when Penny was about to give up in frustration, they came upon an old cage elevator.

"That thing looks like it's about to fall apart," Cisco remarked.

Penny used her stolen ID on the black sensor beside her. The elevator sprang to life with a shuddering groan. "It'll be fine," she told him. "This is a world-class facility…probably."

The metal grate parted when the elevator reached them. Penny hopped in, then grabbed Cisco's arm to drag him in too. "Look, this is so cliché my eyes are about to roll out of my head," she assured him. "Creepy old elevator that leads down to a cold and dripping basement level where they run creepy experiments on their prisoners? That's so overdone it's almost boring."

"It's boring in b-grade action movies." Cisco stabbed the button for the bottom level. "Not so much when you're *in* it."

The floor trembled and began to lower. Penny took the time to check her body cam and quickly scroll through her phone.

Amelia had texted.

I'm just gonna assume you're doing something REALLY important. I called Crenel, he said he'll find Boots. Where the hell are you, Penny?

Climbing a tree to rescue our lame duck.

Penny pressed send to her reply, hoping Amelia would get the reference. Back in first semester, Penny rescued an injured Trevor from a tree. It shouldn't take much for Amelia to connect the dots and realize Penny was on a mission to save him now, but that she couldn't risk tipping off the goons if Amelia's phone was tapped.

The elevator jerked to a stop, and Penny pulled back the metal barrier. The basement looked much like the upper level, though somehow gloomier. The gleaming white floors didn't shine as brightly and the lights overhead held just a hint of yellow. They flickered when Penny and Cisco stepped out of the elevator.

"He must be down here," Penny said in a low voice. "Come on."

The corridor ahead was lined with doors. Penny stopped to peer into the first room, holding her flashlight up to shine through the small glass window.

The room was dark except for a sliver of light from a glowing panel that highlighted a cluster of X-ray images. The details it revealed made little sense to Penny. Rather than bones, it showed solid rods and limbs with too many joints.

She moved the beam of light around until it rested on a white hospital bed. Tall stands held bags of fluid linked to the prone figure on the bed by numerous lengths of plastic tubing. Next to the bed, a heart monitor flatlined.

Penny stretched onto her toes to try and see who was on the bed. She reached the light up, trying to angle it between machines.

"Holy… what?" The mutilated face stared back at her with one lifeless eye. Swollen lips, stitched at the corners, wrapped around a breathing tube and several thin cords attached to the creature's forehead with white adhesive patches.

Penny ran her flashlight down the length of the body. The lumpy mass didn't look at all human. A dangling limb confirmed her guess. Instead of fingers, a translucent flipper peeked out from under the white cloth that covered the rest of the body.

"It's not Trevor," Penny said. She swallowed hard, unsure if relief or horror would win out. "Let's go."

CHAPTER TWENTY-TWO

Trusting her instincts—or possibly because of impossible optimism—Penny didn't stop to look in any of the other rooms. Instead, she went straight to the end of the corridor.

The door it led to was different from the others. "It's a retinal scanner." Cisco pressed a few numbers but the keypad gave a loud beep and an LED flashed red. "What next?"

"You've got to be kidding me!" Penny slammed a hand against the locked door. "This has to be where they're keeping him. Dammit!"

"Here, let's get this off." Cisco used a pair of bolt cutters on the padlock. "Maybe we can shoot through the door."

"Cisco, you *know* that doesn't work." Penny wondered if Jessie knew anything that would help them crack the code. She drew her phone out to message her.

"Penny, come on. Real sewers don't look like that." Cisco pointed back down the corridor. "Brand new buildings don't have elevators like that. *Nothing* in this place follows the rules we're used to."

Penny frowned, then nodded. "Fine. Give it a go, but for crying out loud, don't shoot yourself."

She took cover, pressing against a doorway a short distance back from the door. Cisco stepped back and aimed his gun.

Snap. Snap. Snap.

The Academy-issued silencer didn't entirely eliminate the noise, but Penny knew her ears would be bleeding if he hadn't used it. To her shock, the door swung open.

"See?" Cisco gave her a cocky grin. "Action hero, right here." He flexed a bicep, then pushed the door farther open.

"Trevor!" Penny dashed in, recognizing their friend.

Trevor was strapped to a chair. A metal band locked his head in place, and he stared at a TV screen. His eyes were glazed and his mouth slack. A drip ran from his arm to a bag of clear fluid suspended behind him and sensors attached to his chest linked to a machine that showed his heart rate, slow and fluttering.

"Has he been drugged?" Cisco immediately set to work unstrapping Trevor's arms and legs.

Penny examined the drip. "I don't know what this is." The sticker on the bag was labeled with a series of numbers and letters, but nothing she recognized.

Unlatching the metal band, Cisco attempted to help Trevor stand. "Come on, buddy. We've gotta get you out of here."

Trevor mumbled something incoherent. When Cisco tried to prop him up, Trevor flopped back down, his body limp.

"Can you carry him?" Penny carefully removed the IV, leaving the cannula in place for now.

"Not if I need to shoot something at the same time." Cisco turned worried eyes her way. "Do you think you can cover us both?"

"We haven't been found yet," Penny pointed out. "And we sure as hell can't leave him here."

"We could call for backup?" Cisco grabbed Trevor around the waist and lifted him in a fireman's carry.

"What if this place disappears while we're inside it?" Penny shuddered. "No thanks, I'd rather take my chances with the goons."

"That's your answer, then." Cisco hefted Trevor up onto his shoulder. "Come on. He's a lightweight, but I don't want to haul his ass around forever."

Penny quickly checked her body cam. It was still on. She found the little green light to be a comfort in the dim room. A glance at her phone showed she still had a signal—weak, but there. Nodding, she pulled her gun out and disengaged the safety. "Move out."

Cisco followed on Penny's heels, letting her hold the door open for him before she jumped ahead to take point. When they reached the elevator, Penny blew out a long breath of relief. "Just gotta get to the dock," she murmured.

The elevator ground to a halt on the ground floor. The crisp white lights made her blink. Then, they switched off.

A klaxon blared and the lights flicked back on, red and pulsating.

"They know we're here," Penny snapped. "Let's go." Gun pointed ahead, Penny ran in a low crouch.

Footsteps pounded down the hallway between the

whoops of the alarm, and a guard rounded the corner. Penny took him down with two shots.

"Man down, man down!" someone shouted.

The yell echoed, and Penny cursed.

"I should have let him get closer," she snapped. "So they didn't see him go down."

"He's carrying a machine gun," Cisco called. "I'm kinda glad you didn't."

"Take cover." Penny ignored Cisco's protest. She knew he'd find a way to keep Trevor safe. She dropped to one knee to face off with the team of goons headed their way.

Three men jumped out, firing a smattering of bullets that whizzed over her head and chipped at the wall behind her.

Snap. Snap. Snap. All three crumpled to the ground.

"What are they, Stormtroopers?" Cisco yelled.

"I take it that means you guys are okay?" Penny called.

Cisco chuckled. "Fine, for now. Let's go." He waved her on, the movement throwing eerie shadows in the pulsing red lights.

Penny ran forward, taking down one more guard who had made the mistake of calling for backup over his radio. He reeled as two bullets hit him in the throat, cutting off his cry for help. "Sorry, mate."

Penny pressed up against a wall by the next corner. She held her gun close, then spun and dropped to a knee, pointing it down the corridor.

Her heart stopped. At least a dozen suited men stood in a tight formation at the other end of the hall, guns pointed her way. Penny's eyes dropped to her chest, where a cluster of red dots swayed on her shirt. "Don't shoot!" she yelled.

Slowly, she moved her weapon aside, pointing at the wall as she clicked the safety back on. She let the gun dangle from a finger for a moment, then tossed it out of reach.

The alarms ceased abruptly. Blinking under the bright, white lights, Penny clenched her jaw. *You've got one chance, girl.*

"I need to speak to your boss," she called.

"Why?" One of the guards called back. His voice was hard and precise, exactly what she'd expect from a highly trained government operative. "So you can beg for your life?"

"No," Penny said evenly. "Because he's going to tell you to let us go."

After a brief moment of silence, one man stepped forward from the back. He was a little taller than the others, a little smoother with his slicked-back hair and black wraparound sunglasses. "And why would I do that, Ms. Hingston?"

"As much as I'd like to pretend it's because you recognize that kidnapping young men and stalking women is creepy as hell and you regret it," Penny told him, hand on one hip as she recognized the man. "That's not it."

The Myther Agent didn't respond, just twitched one eyebrow ever so slightly over his shades.

"This is the second time I've found your secret base," Penny continued. "And this time, I know what you're hiding. Those creatures you're experimenting on down there? Highly illegal. The kidnappings? Also illegal." She spread her hands apologetically. "And letting a mere civilian in to see it all? You *know* that's against regulation."

"What makes you think anyone will ever know you were here, or what you found?" The agent raised his gun and pointed it at Penny.

"You'll shoot me to keep it quiet?" Penny asked smoothly.

The agent gave a single, brisk nod. "Don't waste my time, Hingston. You have thirty seconds to convince me not to make you disappear forever."

"The Witchly Web." Penny tossed the phrase at him carelessly. "Dot com," she added after a beat.

Agent Shades pursed his lips, then uttered the URL into his radio.

"You know, they've made a lot of progress on handhelds since the eighties." Penny tapped the radio clipped to her shoulder strap. "Smaller, lighter, and harder to—"

"Uhh, boss?" The voice that crackled over the Shades' radio held more than a hint of worry. "We got a problem. A really big problem."

"What is it, Reid?" Shades kept his flawless composure, speaking in a bored tone.

"You're on the internet," Reid replied.

"What?" Shades flushed and darted a fast look around. "What do you mean?"

"Oh, he's probably referring to the livestream." Penny tapped the tiny body cam below her radio. "Our whole trip through your facility, videoed and streamed to the world wide web. Go on, ask your guy how many people are watching."

Shades, face red and voice tight, did just that. "Reid? What's the damage?"

"Forty-two hundred viewers, boss." The radio crackled

and Reid spoke again. "Twelve have shared it across their social platforms. Oh. *Oh.*"

"Oh, *what*, Reid?" Shades growled.

"That brings the total number of viewers to around ninety-two thousand, sir. Uh, ninety-three. Ninety-five. Sir, I believe we've gone what they call 'viral.'"

"You're exposed, mate." Penny grinned. "A video like that? It'll cross the world in minutes. There's not a shadow left on earth deep enough to hide you and your men."

"Issue a Code Nineteen," Shades barked. "Passcode 7-9-9-alpha-bravo-romeo-0-4-1-tango-1." He slammed the radio unit to the ground, and it shattered. Turning to his men, he yelled, "Stand down. I repeat, stand down. Enact Sudden Death Protocol."

As the unit opposing Penny straightened and strapped their guns away, a robotic voice sounded overhead. "Code Nineteen. Repeat, Code Nineteen. Sudden Death Protocol Enacted. All agents, prepare to evacuate. Code Nineteen."

The team of agents trotted away, leaving their boss alone. Penny unhooked her body cam and switched it off.

"Seems you're letting us go after all, Agent," Penny said. "I have something to offer you, though."

"You've just dismantled our entire operation." Shades held up a good front, but Penny could see his weariness. "Twenty years I've worked for this department. They'll shut us down by sunup."

Penny took a step closer. The man might be a Myther, but in some ways, she felt sorry for him. "Do me a favor," she said. "One favor. It's a big one, though. Do it, and I'll tell them you wiped my memory, that I don't remember anything. You know the body cam will only have caught so much."

Shades straightened, a hint of his earlier determination returning. "What is it?"

Penny grinned. "It's a rescue mission."

CHAPTER TWENTY-THREE

Penny stared at Agent Crenel, bleary-eyed and exhausted.

"What do you mean you don't remember?" His frown was so deep Penny wondered if it would leave a permanent set of wrinkles.

"I just...don't." She shrugged. "I'm telling the truth, Agent."

And she *was*, as much as Agent Crenel wanted to believe otherwise. Her last memory was of leaving the Twisted Monkey. She vividly recalled the orange lights of the bar dimming to soft moonlight, and the chill of the open air touching her skin as she stepped outside. Then? Not a damn thing.

Crenel threw his hands in the air. "Fine! Fine. Nothing I can do about it, right? Banks is going to think I've gone senile, but hey! The whole world is crazy now, right?"

He threw the thin file on his desk.

"Well, Trevor did come out alive," Penny pointed out.

"As far as we know, no one got hurt. I may not remember what I did, but I'm pretty sure it was *spectacular*."

Boots hissed in agreement. She looked no worse for wear after her strange arrival in a watertight box, dropped by the Academy door next to a trussed-up Professor Steele.

"Just like a turkey," the dean remarked before explaining that according to what she and Amelia had pieced together from security footage, the professor had kidnapped Boots and was on her way to the airport with a one-way ticket to New Zealand.

No one knew exactly how Steele had been caught or who had delivered the pair to the Academy. Penny had her suspicions, but they were just that. Certainly, there wasn't enough proof to indulge Crenel with her theory. After all, it sounded entirely mad.

"Oh, spectacular, I'm sure." Crenel finally lit the cigarette dangling from his mouth, only to hastily stub it out in an ashtray hidden in his drawer when the door to his office opened.

"Do I look like an idiot?" Dean March wore a look of well-worn patience. "I can smell it from here."

"You said you'd better not see me," Crenel began.

"Yes, yes." March waved him off impatiently. "Your friends would like to see you, Penny. Do you feel up to it?"

Penny jumped to her feet, almost dropping Boots in her haste. "Hell, yes." She'd been locked in Crenel's office for almost two hours.

"Well, then, unless you're under arrest?" She cocked an eyebrow at her husband, who scowled back and plucked a new cigarette from his packet. March sighed and shook her head but stayed silent as she gently closed the door after Penny.

"Thanks for the rescue," Penny told her as Boots made herself comfortable on her shoulders. "Any word on Trevor?"

"Perfectly healthy," Dean March replied. "But, like you and Cisco, he has no memory of the events that occurred."

"Oh." Penny wondered if she'd ever know what had gone on after the video feed had cut off. "Where are they?"

"In your room." Dean March pointed toward the hallway Penny would need to take to get there. "Take care, dear."

"You too, Dean March." Penny walked quickly, Boots wriggling to show her own excitement.

Unlike when she'd left, the room was spotless—except for the cluster of people sprawled on the floor and draped over beds. Amelia, Cisco, Red, Trevor, and Jessie all looked up as she entered.

"There she is!" Amelia quickly moved over to give Penny room to sit on her bed. "I can't believe the old bastard grilled you for so long!"

"At least he's got it out of his system," Penny told her gratefully. "He's closed the case, so I won't have to put up with any more questions. That means I can ask, what in the hell did I *do* in there?"

Penny had seen the bodycam footage—she and half the world, it seemed. It had been a surreal experience to hear her own voice and even catch glimpses of her reflection all kitted out in her assault gear when she had no memory of what had happened.

The footage itself wasn't what bothered her, it was what

came after. And before. "How in the hells did I patch a bodycam into a blog?" she asked. Her eyes slipped to Jessie. "Did you have something to do with that?"

Jessie flicked her hand up, examining her nails. "That serum really did a number on you, huh?"

"Serum?" Penny frowned. "I don't remember—"

"Because it was an amnesia serum, dummy!" Jessie rolled onto her knees. "After the bodycam switched off, you made a deal with Mister Matrix. You said you'd pretend you forgot everything you saw if he did you a favor."

"What favor?" Penny already had a hunch, but Jessie was clearly enjoying her role as an informant.

"You told him how your friend got nabbed by some crazy lady. If he tracked down Steele and Boots, you wouldn't respond to any questions." Jessie grinned proudly.

"And instead of trusting my word, he made me take the serum," Penny finished. "Damn. I was really dumb. What if he hadn't come through?"

"Oh, you already knew I was listening," Jessie explained. "You called me before you went in. You gave me Amelia's login details—"

"Which I've already changed," Amelia pointed out.

"And asked me to patch the cam stream to her live channel," Jessie finished. "Also, Amelia, you *really* need a better password. K9sRhot2020? I cracked that in under half a minute."

Amelia glowed red and mumbled something about nosey teenagers.

Cisco had watched the exchange in awe. "I don't

remember *any* of that. Penny, did you really set all that up? You're a freaking genius!"

Jessie's jaw dropped, outrage written all over her face. "What am I, a pork chop?"

"I mean, you're *both* geniuses. Genii?" Cisco shook his head. "You're both *really* clever."

"Of course we are," Jessie stated primly. "We're girls."

"You're forgetting who found *Polybius* in the first place." Trevor still looked a little pale, but otherwise well. "Who *knows* how many people they might have kidnapped and experimented on if I hadn't?"

"Yeah, well, you're not like other boys." Jessie smirked at Trevor, whose white cheeks immediately turned scarlet.

"Hold up," Amelia interrupted. "Do you two have a *thing* going on?"

"Yes," Jessie replied as Trevor mumbled, "No!"

Jessie rolled her eyes. "We're still working out the details."

"You dawg." Cisco shoved Trevor, misjudging his friend's balance and sending him sprawling on the floor. "Uh, sorry."

Penny ignored the withering glare Jessie shot at Cisco. "So what about Boots? Crenel told me she'd been dropped off at the door, but he wasn't exactly forthcoming with information."

"That is a whole other story," Amelia told her, eyes sparkling. "Steele was trying to flee the country! Crenel told me that she was delivered back to us with a full suitcase and her passport and plane ticket glued to her forehead."

"Oh, Boots." The thought of losing her friend tore at Penny's heart. "I'm so, so sorry."

Boots butted her face against Penny's chin.

Amelia brushed off Penny's concern. "Crenel had flagged Steele's passport moments before she appeared. If she'd made the flight, she'd have stepped off the plane in New Zealand to an arrest warrant."

"Thank you." Penny wrapped an arm around Amelia. "I'm sorry for putting you in that position. Did you figure out what my message meant?"

Amelia nodded. "You're nowhere near as bad as Cisco at secret codes."

"Hey!" Cisco straightened. "I… okay, that's actually a really fair point." He shot Jessie a salty glare. "We can't all be geniuses. Some of us have to be strong, handsome, and an expert at romance."

Red snorted at that, but Amelia tossed a pillow at his head. "She got music, a candlelit dinner, and a *water sprite performance* for her first date. I got dirt in my underpants."

"I hate you, Cisco," Red grumbled. "I really, really hate you."

Chuckling, Penny threw a pillow at Cisco. "I told you he would."

Cisco caught the pillow, grinning. "Just you wait and see what I've got planned for our next date. He'll never speak to me again!"

Penny leaned back and sighed. "I'm just glad we'll have time. It's still a couple of weeks until exams start. Surely we won't get any more missions allocated this semester. It'll be cruisey until the end."

A knock on the door interrupted her happy sigh. "Come in?"

Agent Crenel stuck his head through the door. "Good. You're all here."

"Why?" The relief Penny had felt mere seconds before evaporated.

"There's a mission. One you'll be perfect for." His eyes locked on Penny as he spoke.

"Me?" she asked. "Why me?"

"Bunyip outbreak."

"Bunyips?" Penny squeaked. "In America?"

"Nope." Crenel grinned. "Pack your bags, kid. You're going home."

THE END

You may have noticed there's a LOT of history in these books. Tiny glimpses, yes — there is sooo much more to Bacchus than party god and bartender — but I've loved digging through old legends, ghost hunting sites, mythology books and spam letters.

Yeah, old Prince and his shifty lawyer are 100% my favourite characters in these books :D And, they spurred the idea for Polybius. I was looking for something a little different from the usual ancient legends. I believe history isn't just in the past. We create it, every day. Computers and tech are forming a larger part of our culture all the time, and this book celebrates it.

Also, the Stranger Things arcade scenes are wicked as.

And, I know the more off-the-wall my weird ideas are, the higher chance there is of making Michael snort coke all over his computer screen.

I mean, how else do you calculate the success of a series other than ruined keyboards and burning nostrils?

I hope you're enjoying Penny and Boots, and I REALLY

hope you love the next installment. No spoilers, but...
we're going on a trip!

See you then,

Amy

P.S. STILL salty about Diego. I will carry this to my
grave.

First, thank you for not only reading this story, but reading these author notes as well!

I will have to admit that the first time I read a story using Bacchus as a character, he was a disgusting character with no redeeming values and I hated him.

But that was many years and hundreds of books ago. And I am glad Amy decided to flavor the god differently.

I am also glad to see that I can be mature enough to give Bacchus a second chance.

KEYBOARDS AND BURNING NOSTRILS

So, Amy can be blisteringly funny. However to have her admit that she is using this talent for evil is just horrible. Well, it's horrible if you are the person she is trying to attack. I mean, have you felt Coke coming out of your nostrils?

It stings like a $&@)?!!

Then again, I try to time funny comments when Zen

Master Steve™ and I are on a Zoom call and he is taking a sip of his coffee...

<Editor's note> I try to time my funny comments on Zoom calls so not only does coffee come out Steve's nose, but both their heads hit the desk in disbelief at the same time.

I guess turnabout is fair play.

Damn, I can't drink when reading Amy's books.

Take care and I look forward to chatting in another book!

Ad Aeternitatem,

Michael

www.ingramcontent.com/pod-product-compliance
Lightning Source LLC
Chambersburg PA
CBHW050254110726

47898CB00007B/2401